MW01115878

# Argenis
## Fated Dragon Daddies
### Book 2

## Pepper North

Pepper North
With a Wink Publishing, LLC

# Author's Note:

The following story is completely fictional. The characters are all over the age of 18 and as adults choose to live their lives in an age play environment.

This is a series of books that can be read in any order. You may, however, choose to read them sequentially to enjoy the characters best. Subsequent books will feature characters that appear in previous novels as well as new faces.

You can contact me on
my <u>Pepper North</u> Facebook pages,
at <u>www.4peppernorth.club</u>
eMail at <u>4peppernorth@gmail.com</u>
I'm experimenting with <u>Instagram</u>, <u>Twitter</u>, and <u>Tiktok</u>.
Come join me everywhere!

Nestled in the center of a ring of imposing mountains, the city of Wyvern has existed for hundreds of years. Its quaint town center wraps around a square featuring a commanding dragon statue elevated on a block-wide platform for all to admire. The names chiseled into the risers of the stone steps are a mystery to most. Many feature the last names of the founding families of the town without explanation. During the prosperity of technological tools, most forgot the old ways.

One female descendant of each founding family has traditionally served as the keeper of knowledge. Passing a huge tome from generation to generation, that woman knows of the pact the original settlers made with the first inhabitants of this land. The agreement between the huge, lethal creatures living in the mountain tops and the struggling, besieged humans sealed the duties for both sides. Most of the citizens of Wyvern have forgotten this pact, occupied by the hustle and bustle of modern life. But the long lives of the dragons ensure they have not forgotten that it promises protection for the people and fated mates for the dragons until the end of time.

When all things powered by technology suddenly cease to function, the worst features of humanity erupt as people struggle to survive. Once again, the strength and power of the massive beasts who have guarded the city is needed. Revealing themselves once again to the masses, the horde of dragons fulfills their promise.

As descendants of those original families are found, mate bonds are forged between dragons and humans. The old ways are essential to the survival of all, and the ancient pact will soar in importance once again. For there are dragons, and they hunt for more than just prey.

Drake, the most powerful dragon in the horde has found his mate amid the growing population of Wyvern. Others still search, hoping that each day brings their mate back to their ancestors' home. The stakes are dire. One teeters on the brink of being lost without the companionship of his mate.

# Chapter 1

"I'm going to open the door to get some fresh air," Ciel said hesitantly. The man in the driver's seat was becoming angrier by the moment when he couldn't figure out what was going on with his car.

"Just get out of the car," her Uber driver ordered. "Call for another ride."

They'd already sat in the vehicle for fifteen minutes and it had become quite toasty inside.

"My phone isn't working. Is yours?" she asked.

"If it was, do you think I'd just be sitting here?" he asked, completely pissed off and annoyed.

Ciel pulled the door handle, but it wouldn't open. He must have the child locks engaged so no one could stiff him for a job. She waited for him to connect the dots and realize she couldn't get out. Pressing a button with barely concealed anger, the driver glared at her in the rearview mirror. She tried again. Nothing.

When he finally got out of the car and opened the back door, Ciel quickly slid out of the seat. She turned around and pulled the release on the seatback to fold it down and dragged her suitcase out of the trunk before he could get mad about it not opening either. Thank goodness a friend had the same model.

Dragging her suitcase up on the sidewalk, Ciel started walking. She had no idea where she was. Totally dependent on her phone's GPS, she'd never learned street names other than the main drags of the town where she went to college. When she passed a grocery store, she made herself stop and walk in so she could get directions.

The employees were all seated on the counters at the checkouts, enjoying popsicles. One met her gaze and invited, "All the frozen food is melting. The manager is giving away anything you want to take with you."

"Really?" Ciel double checked.

"Yeah. No charge. He's going to have to throw it out anyway," the cashier told her.

"I really came in for directions. Could someone tell me how to get to Washington Boulevard?" Ciel asked.

"Sure. I live near there. It's seventeen blocks that way and then turn left and go three more blocks." He turned to his coworkers to say, "I don't know how I'm getting home. That's too far to walk."

Looking enviously at the icy treat in their hands, Ciel asked, "Can I get a popsicle? I have money."

"It's on us. The cash registers aren't working. Go grab a couple of things," another cashier urged.

From the grins on their faces, they were enjoying giving items away. Ciel shrugged and walked into the store. She grabbed a lime popsicle from an open box and debated. What could serve as a meal if she didn't get home for dinner? Peanut butter and jelly snack sandwiches looked at her. Those would work. She grabbed some chocolate muffins for dessert. If they were going to be thrown out, why not?

The employees just waved as she walked back to the front with her items. She hesitated in the doorway. "Could I get a bottle of water?"

"You'd have to pay for that."

Ciel found two dollars in her phone wallet and handed it over. Grabbing the biggest bottle of water from the rapidly warming display case, she wheeled her suitcase outside. There was an empty bench about a half a block down. Ciel stopped and ate her popsicle, leaning forward so the quickly melting mixture dripped onto the concrete.

What was going on? Her phone still wasn't working. How had the manager of the store known that the power wouldn't come back on? She'd had some strange lapses in connectivity with her phone and laptop over the last few days. Maybe this area had been hit harder?

Ciel shrugged. It didn't really matter.

Glancing up and down the street, she noticed more and more people gathering in the street among the non-operational cars. No one even tried to move them out of the road now. A young man rode by on his bike and Ciel couldn't help being envious. Those wheels were working at least.

After finishing her frozen treat, Ciel felt better. She wiped her fingers on her pants and licked at a sticky spot, finally splashing some water on her hands when she couldn't free herself from the limey mixture. She took a quick drink and tried to figure out what to do.

Obviously, there was nothing else to do but start walking. Catching sight of her strappy sandals, Ciel knew she couldn't walk four blocks in those without wearing blisters on her toes and heels. She opened her suitcase and pulled out her sneakers and a pair of socks. The heat made her wish she could change into shorts, but there was no place to do that now. Hopefully, she'd find a bathroom.

After swapping footwear, she tucked her sandals away and squeezed in the food she now had. She zipped the suitcase again and slid her bottle into the front pocket before standing. This couldn't last forever. If she got to Washington Boulevard, she could catch a taxi or rideshare to the train station.

Her mom had to be going crazy. She'd blown a gasket when Ciel had chosen to attend the state university several towns away. Thank goodness none of her mom's worries about her being harmed in the big city had come true.

*Is this happening in Wyvern?* The image of the giant dragon in the town's center square popped into her head. That would be better than a bike. Laughter spurted through her lips at the preposterous idea of riding a massive beast through the air. *Fables and fairytales.*

## Chapter 2

Argenis spotted her. An attractive woman about forty-five standing in the crowd at the square. There was something more than just concern about what had stopped all the technology—more than a concern about dragons.

After the mayor had dispersed the group into useful categories, he'd watched that woman and followed. When she stopped to talk to Aurora about a missing person, Argenis had acted.

"I will handle this one," he told Aurora firmly, and took the paper gently from her hand.

He saw Aurora look at Drake. He met the gold dragon's eyes solidly. As he suspected, Drake understood. Aurora's mate nodded, and she relaxed.

"Of course. Here's her mother. Would you like to ask her any questions?" Aurora asked, gesturing at the woman in front of her.

"Yes," Argenis confirmed succinctly and walked a short distance away.

"Follow him," Aurora suggested, pointing at the silver dragon.

He kept his face expressionless as the woman leaned in to whisper, "Is it safe? He won't eat me, will he?"

Argenis could see the amusement that flashed across Aurora's lovely face before she relieved the woman's doubts. "You're perfectly safe. Tell him everything you can to help him find your daughter."

"Thank you, miss." The woman hesitated and then asked, "Are you happy? You know, being with a dragon?"

"More than I ever thought was possible," Aurora assured her. "Go talk to him."

"Shouldn't I stay with the others who are worried about someone outside of Wyvern?" she asked, wavering between nervousness in talking to a dragon and worrying about missing out on having help with her daughter.

"The missing Wyvern reports filed with that group over there will be prioritized, and dragons will be asked to investigate those deemed most urgent. If you wish to be somewhere in line for help, that's where you should be. If you wish to have a dragon's help, here and now..." Argenis let his voice drift away as she digested his message.

"Oh, please. I would love to have your help immediately. I meant no disrespect," she said hastily before adding, "It's my daughter Ciel."

She searched in her pocket and withdrew a photo. "I searched for a picture to bring. We've kept so many on our phones in the last few years. The most recent printed one I could find is this one—from her high school graduation. She's a couple of years older now."

She handed Argenis a high school graduation picture of a young woman leaning against the dragon statue just across the square. He swallowed hard, controlling his visible reaction.

"Ciel is a very sweet person. She'll know that I'm

worrying and will try to get home. With no transportation, I'm worried someone will take advantage of her.... Maybe hurt her."

"Where was she when you talked to her last?" Argenis forced himself to focus.

"She was in her dorm room, cramming for her last final. Ciel told me she was packed and would call me from the train station when she got there. I don't suppose the trains are still running. They don't use technology, do they?"

Argenis didn't even acknowledge that question. Everything used technology now. It made life easier for everyone. "What university?"

"Oh. Sorry. She's at the state university in the capital."

"Got it. You think she'd head to the train station first?" Argenis asked.

"Yes. Then she'd start walking. I don't even know if she has the roads memorized. We drove her back and forth a few times, but she was always on her phone," Maureen admitted.

He could hear her feelings of helplessness in her tone. "Thank you. I will do my best to locate her and bring her back. Tell me something that only you would know. That way, she'll know she can trust me."

"Her childhood toy was a stuffed dragon. She still sleeps with it. Ciel wouldn't leave the store until I bought it. She never acted like that. I tried to get her to like the bronze colored one because I was worried the silver would get dirty."

The dragon inside Argenis roared his disapproval. He did not like the thought of Ciel with a different colored stuffie. Argenis retained control with an ironclad force. "Little girls know what they need sometimes."

"She took such good care of Silly. He was in the bathtub with her frequently."

Argenis felt his dragon nod with satisfaction. He thoroughly approved of this. "Silly was the toy's name?"

"Yes. Short for silver. She still talks to him as if he were a real dragon. I warned her about taking a child's stuffed animal to college. I didn't want people to get the wrong idea."

His temper flared, as well as his nostrils. How could this woman not know enough about her child? He reminded himself that she was there and worried. She hadn't just sat at home, sending random thoughts out into the universe. She'd pushed herself to come to the meeting. His dragon huffed and settled down.

Memorizing the photograph, Argenis handed it back to Ciel's mother. "I will bring her home."

"You can keep that. I have more. And thank you."

Stalking away without another word, Argenis folded the paper and placed it and the photo carefully in his pocket. He sent the dragons a mental blast.

*I am off to hunt down a Wyvern citizen.*

Their communication over the years had dwindled. Those dusty connections had revitalized over the last few days.

*What made you choose this one?*

The angry tone of the black dragon echoed in his mind. Argenis shook his head. The solitude caused by surviving without a mate had changed Keres. He tempered his retort to not respond with the same emotion. He did not want Ciel's existence to be tainted by negativity.

*This one is my mate.*

Silence followed for several heartbeats as Argenis strode to a wide section of the town that would allow him to release his dragon. He did not add his apologies to Keres for having found his mate first. That wasn't how it worked.

*My congratulations.*

The weary response made Argenis incline his head down slightly. He, like the others, grieved for Keres's loss. Someday. "My congratulations as well," Khadar, the emerald dragon, chimed in and the others echoed his good wishes. *I will return with her as quickly as possible. Call me in an emergency. I will respond if it doesn't put my mate in danger.*

With the message sent, Argenis allowed the change to flow over him. The feeling of power and heightened senses never failed to flood his mind and form with energy. Now with an urgent mission, he felt back in his element.

Argenis roared a warning for villagers too close to get away and waited for several seconds. Powering upward with his muscular hind legs, Argenis took to the sky. He heard the shouts of the village kids in awe of his dragon form. The toy shop off the square had sold out of the dragons they had in stock when the demand skyrocketed.

*Being a dragon is cool again,* he thought and allowed himself to dive toward the building tops to thrill his onlookers.

Focusing on the woman who awaited him, Argenis set a path for the capital. He was concerned by the chaos on the ground below him now more than ever. It had not taken everyone long to figure out that the technology grid wasn't just down. It was obliterated. Compounding the confusion and violent feedback with no instant communication systems, people felt abandoned and desperate.

Rioting and lawlessness were growing. People had begun to stockpile essentials and defensive materials. His dragon vision was extremely fine-tuned and didn't require him to fly close to see the actions on land. Grateful that his mate was close, Argenis sped up his pace. The faster he found her, the better.

# Chapter 3

"Hey! What do you have in the suitcase?"

She kept her gaze on the man. He looked scruffy and unkempt. Over the last twenty-four hours, Ciel had grown increasingly concerned. The changes from interacting with the kind people in the grocery store to the growing desperation of the public milling around made her walk as fast as possible. Hopefully when she got out of town, she would feel less nervous.

An hour ago, she'd tried to buy an extra bottle of water from a man pushing a wheelbarrow down the street. He'd just laughed and told her she'd have to steal some for herself.

"Money won't buy anything now. It's worthless." When he drew back the edge of his shirt, the handle of the gun in his waistband made her back away.

Sleeping last night... Sleeping was a wild exaggeration. She'd walked until she couldn't go any further. Finally, she'd pushed her suitcase into a thicket of bushes and crawled after it. Trying not to think of the creatures who might lurk there, she hoped the greenery would provide her protection from the human predators. She'd caught a few catnaps between jerking awake at scary sounds.

Thank goodness for her frozen food choices. The peanut butter and jelly crustless sandwiches provided some protein and sugar for energy. The chocolate muffins? Reassurance.

When dawn broke, she fought her way out of the shrubs. Feeling awful, she took advantage of a broken store door to grab two more bottles of water, but left everything else. At the last minute, she walked to the liquor store's register, intending to leave money. The buzzing of flies made her look over the counter.

She fled to the street, tears pouring down her face. Quickly, Ciel wiped those away and made herself stop. Losing water wasn't an option. Who knew when she'd find more? Shaking her head, she wondered how people had just become savages.

Nearing the train station a couple of hours later, she looked down the road leading to the tracks. There was no sound, except for a few loud shouts. She hesitated for only a few seconds before continuing on the main street to the highway. It looked like her feet were the only thing she could count on.

A few hours later, she dragged her suitcase off the pavement and headed for a clump of trees to rest and cool off. After dropping to the ground, she looked at her hands and hissed. Despite swapping the suitcase between her hands, Ciel had blisters on her palms.

The sound of wheels on the pavement made her look up. A man weaved between the now stationary cars on a bike with a small trailer. Feeling apprehensive, Ciel scrambled on her hands and knees to hide behind a tree.

"I can see you, girl." The man's rough voice grated on her ears.

"I don't want any trouble," she called back.

"A young woman alone is the perfect victim. Give me everything you have, and I'll leave you alone." He swung his leg over the seat as he dismounted from the bike.

"What do you want with jeans and T-shirts? I don't think they'll fit," Ciel tried to distract him with humor as she scrambled to her feet.

"Everything will sell to someone."

"I'm not just going to give you my things because you're a bully."

"And I asked nicely. I have no problem hurting you if that's what it takes," he stated in a hard voice as he stalked forward.

"I just want you to leave me alone," Ciel protested and abandoned the safety of the tree to grab the handle of her bag and started running. The large case bashed into her legs and calves as it bounced through the tall grass.

A strong yank on the suitcase threw her off balance. Ciel fell backward, knocking the breath out of her lungs. He didn't say anything else but simply ripped the handle out of her hand and lugged the suitcase up the hill toward his bike.

*Silly!*

As soon as she could gather herself, Ciel scrambled up after him. "You can't take that. It's got things in it I need." She didn't care about anything else.

"Medicine will sell, too."

"No. It's not medicine. Just let me get something from inside and you can have it," Ciel begged.

"Too late." He tossed the suitcase on the pile in the cart and jumped on the bike.

Rushing forward, she tried to pull the suitcase off the pile. A glint of metal made her jump back. Ciel stared at the man, who now wielded a large knife already stained with some dark substance.

"If I get off this bike again, it will be to carve you into a decoration that I will leave on the side of the road to bleed out. Is this how you want to die?"

Horrified, she stepped further back as her self-preservation kicked in. He wasn't exaggerating. Silly popped into her mind. "Please, sir. I just want my childhood stuffie."

"Time to grow up, bitch. Be thankful you're still alive."

She watched him pedal away. Dashing back down the hill, she grabbed the bottle of water she'd dropped in the grass. Unable to give up, Ciel followed him. *I'm coming, Silly.*

A dark cloud covered the sun and Ciel looked up, thankful for the break from the sun beating down on her. She'd lost track of the man a couple of hours ago. Unable to give up on reuniting with Silly, she kept walking.

When the cloud moved quickly, she glanced up. *What the...* Even her thoughts froze in her mind at the enormous beast circling above her. *He's not trying to land... Fuck!*

Her heart skipped a beat as if excited, but her mind overruled that reaction. Pulling on the last of her energy, Ciel sprinted away toward the safety of the tree line next to the highway. She heard a heavy thump behind her and swore she felt the ground shiver below her. Reaching the bushes, she tried to dart through them.

"Ah!" she gasped and reeled backward, wrapping her arms around herself after the metal barbs of the hidden fence bit into her skin, ripping her T-shirt.

"Ciel. Stop!"

She whirled around to stare at a handsome man who strode forward toward her. "Where did you come from? I'm losing it. I thought I saw a dragon," Ciel told him, hating the weak tremble she heard in her voice.

Before he could answer, she blurted, "I'm going to fight if you plan to hurt me."

"It's okay, Ciel. I'm one of the good guys. Your mother, Maureen sent me."

"How do I know that's true?" Seeing one cup of her bra showing through the torn fabric of her shirt, Ciel tried to shield herself and grimaced at the smear of blood left on the fabric.

"I know about Silly, Little one."

"Silly?" she repeated, as if she didn't have a clue what he was talking about.

"A silver dragon you wouldn't leave the toy store in Wyvern until your mother bought him."

There was no way he knew about Silly unless someone in her family had told him. She took a deep breath and exhaled, trying to calm her thudding heart.

Studying him, she scanned in his handsome face. She wasn't usually a beard fan, but the facial hair softened his chiseled jawline. And those eyes. The unusual color of ice blue. They seemed to look through her.

"Where did the dragon go?" she asked.

"I'm the dragon, Ciel. I'll fly us back to Wyvern when you're ready," Argenis told her.

"My mom sent a flying lizard to save me?" At this point, Ciel was sure she was hallucinating.

"Dragon."

"Sorry, dragon." That seemed to be important to him.

"Thank you. You were unaware of the dragon guardians of Wyvern?" he asked and seemed to be baffled.

"My grandmother told me stories about them, but I thought it was like a legend," she admitted.

"We did too much to hide ourselves," Argenis said, shaking his head.

"There are more of you? Dragons?"

"Wyvern has nine dragon guardians. There are others scattered around the world."

"How is that not on the evening news?" she asked, pressing one spot on her ribcage that stung. Her hand came away stained with a small amount of blood.

"You hurt yourself, Little one. I will not allow that. It's time to get back so I can tend those wounds," he said, walking forward.

"Are you really here to take me home?" Ciel asked, ignoring his statement. Why would he take care of her?

"Yes. You belong in Wyvern." He placed a hand on the small of her back to help her up to the road.

Once she was there, he stepped back to scan her body. Before she could protest him checking her out, he reached over his head to grab a handful of his shirt. The breath wheezed out of her lungs at the sight of his chiseled chest. Afraid she was making a fool of herself, she tore her gaze away.

"You're bleeding." He used his shirt to wipe her arms clean and dabbed at the injuries revealed by the tear in her shirt and another one in her jeans. "I'm sorry I frightened you, Ciel."

"You only scared part of me," she answered defensively.

"I'm glad, Little one."

After flinging his shirt over his shoulder, Argenis held his hand out for hers. "Let's go home."

When she placed her hand in his, a sharp heat built on

her skin. She pulled her hand free, joking, "Now I know not to touch you. Dragons are hot."

His eyes blazed silver, and he held out his hand again. "You'll be fine now," he assured her.

Ciel tentatively touched his skin and when she felt nothing but normal body heat, she rested her hand fully on his. "Better. I guess I'm lucky you can turn that off."

"The mating heat is normal. It passes after the first touch."

He helped her back up on the road as she considered that statement. "Mating heat?"

"May I explain everything to you when we get back to Wyvern?" he asked.

"Definitely." At home, she could be safe and figure out what was going on. He seemed normal, but...

"Let's head to that cleared space."

His hand pressed against the back of her shirt as he guided her. Ciel instinctively stepped a bit closer, so her arm touched his bare chest. She didn't understand, but she needed the contact. His arm wrapped around her waist and pulled her closer. *Yes. Better.*


"Is it different there?" she asked, to distract herself. Maybe her home would be unaffected.

"It's safe. Technology is gone everywhere."

Ciel shook her head as the reality of how much her world had changed. "I should have skipped finals." Or the last two years, she thought, dejected.

"This is a good place. I'll have you home soon."

His voice was soft and comforting. That one bit of kindness broke her. Tears burst from her eyes as all the struggles of the last twenty-four hours registered on her. She'd even lost her childhood friend. "He took Silly."

"Who took your stuffie?"

"A man on a bike with a trailer. He stole my suitcase and threatened me with a knife."

"I spotted him about three miles in front of you. He'll be further now. Let's go get Silly."

"You'd bother with a stuffed dragon?" she asked, amazed that as the world fell apart, this man—beast—cared.

"Yes, Little one. Come. We'll pick up Silly and head home to take care of you. When I change, step on my front foot and climb up to straddle my neck. You will need to hold on."

# Chapter 4

He felt her gaze follow him into the empty space. How would she react? Concentrating, Argenis called his dragon forth. The internal celebrations of his dragon had challenged his control. When she had touched him and the mating bond linked them together, Argenis had battled the dragon for control.

Stretching his wings, Argenis posed for his mate to impress her. A first impression was important. He swiveled his head to the side to watch her reaction. Pure amazement played over her expressive features.

She walked forward and lifted a hand to touch the scales covering his foreleg. He closed his eyes at the incredible feel of her skin against him. "You like that," she whispered.

He opened one eye to capture her gaze and nod. As their connection matured, he'd be able to speak to her mind to mind when in dragon form. She stroked him again, and he allowed his pleasure to rumble up his throat.

"You purr," she said with delight.

Shaking his head in affront, Argenis disagreed. He was

not a kitten. He snarled a bit to reestablish his place at the top of the food chain.

"Oh! Sorry, big bad dragons don't purr."

He ignored the hint of amusement and swung his neck to gesture to his back. It was time to go.

"Oh, yeah." Quickly, she scrambled up into position. Argenis steadied her with his snout, enjoying the scent of his mate. She was... delectable.

When she held on, he rose to his feet and paused for a moment as she tightened her grasp. Before she could relax, he launched himself into the air. Her squeal of delight was music to his ears.

"I don't know if you can hear me, but this is amazing."

He nodded and turned to wink an eye at her. Scanning the road before them, he looked for the stuffie thief. He wouldn't allow that to happen. He growled when his view spotted the bike. It took several minutes for Ciel to see the man.

"There he is. That's my suitcase."

Argenis couldn't help but notice that her suitcase was silver. He waggled his wings slightly—not enough to make her off balance, but she did tighten her arms around his neck. Gradually going lower, Argenis loved the moment the man felt his presence and looked over his shoulder. The bike rocked back and forth, stabilized only by the cart behind him. He pedaled like a wild man. Like that was going to help him.

Reaching out his forearm, Argenis plucked the silver suitcase from the top of the pile. He allowed his hot breath to float over the man, singeing his hair slightly. Wrinkling his sensitive snout at that smell, Argenis angled back to the sky. He did one loop around to approach the villain one more time. With pinpoint precision, he blasted the contents of the cart, setting everything on fire.

Ciel's cheer was his reward as the man bailed off the bike and then frantically tried to unhook it before the flames damaged the last of his possessions. *Don't mess with a dragon's mate.*

Argenis set a path for Wyvern. He didn't rush. When he got her back to town, they would no longer be alone. He enjoyed having Ciel to himself.

"Argenis?" she yelled into the wind.

He nodded to encourage her.

"This isn't the last time I'll see you, is it?"

His shake of denial was vigorous.

She hugged his neck harder and pressed her cheek to his scales in response. "You do purr!" she shouted in delight when his happiness escaped in a deep rumble.

He chose to pretend he didn't hear that comment.

In a short period of time, he landed in Wyvern. She slid down to stand on the ground but leaned next to him. Gently, he guided her a short distance from his body with a careful sweep of his wing. When he was sure she was safe, he morphed back to human form. Usually there was a subconscious dismay due to the loss of his dragon senses. Now, there was satisfaction in supporting his mate.

She flew instantly to the suitcase and unzipped it. Sliding her hand inside, she searched for something. He could tell the moment her hand closed around her beloved stuffie. Ciel took a deep breath and blew it out in relief.

"Silly's okay."

"Come, Ciel. Let's let everyone know you're safe and get those wounds disinfected." He wrapped his arm around her and guided her the short distance to the square.

Stopping at the first aid tent that the medical team must have erected after he left, Argenis asked for supplies and tended his mate himself. Ciel didn't realize it yet, but the touch of other men would repel her until they were fully mated. When her wounds from the encounter with the barbed wire were treated, he led her from the tent and to a secluded nook. Reaching forward to cup her chin, he raised her eyes to meet his gaze.

"You are so quiet, Little one. Are you okay?"

"Something's happening to me. Inside."

"You feel the heat building. Look at your hand." He watched her lift her hand. Her eyes narrowed as she turned her hand to several angles before meeting his gaze with a surprised expression.

"What is this?" Ciel asked, waving her hand.

"It is the mate mark."

"Mate mark? What's that? It looks like a dragon," she murmured, touching it with her fingertip.

The low moan that Argenis allowed to escape his lips brought her attention back to him. "You felt that?" Ciel tried it again.

Clenching his teeth, Argenis controlled his body's reaction with the strength of his dragon. Wrapping his hand around her hand, he tugged her finger away. "Little one, you are testing my control." He stroked a fingertip across the image to return the temptation.

"Oh. My. Goodness." Her staccato words underlined the impact of his touch.

He gave her a few seconds to recover. When she could finally meet his gaze, Argenis kept himself from smiling. The heat between them was quite remarkable.

"That's the mate heat. It will continue to grow until our union to prevent us from being stubborn and failing to heed its importance."

"Union. Like sex?" she hissed at him.

"Our bond is eons long in the making. Dragons do not

choose a partner casually, as humans do. We wait for our mate to appear. It is impossible to deny one's fated mate."

"Argenis, this is crazy. I can't be your mate. I mean... Not that anything is wrong with you. You're very handsome in both forms. But I never expected to meet a guy who's a dragon."

"You will need to be close to me."

"I don't understand what you are talking about, Argenis. Thank you for rescuing me and Silly. I'll head home now so my mom doesn't worry," Ciel informed him.

"It was my pleasure, Little one."

He watched her grab her suitcase handle and wheel it toward the corner. Her first couple of steps were at a quick pace. The next few were slower and more deliberate. Then Argenis watched her determination kicked in as she struggled to take another step.

When she looked over her shoulder, he could see the pain written on her face. Immediately, he started forward. "You're hurting yourself, Ciel."

"What is happening here?" she asked, on the brink of tears as he joined her.

Argenis gathered her into his arms and held her close. She melted against him. Enchanted, he pressed a kiss to the top of her head. "I am sorry you're fighting this, Little one. I will do what I can to help you, but our bond cannot be broken even if I wanted it gone. Which I do not." That final phrase he emphasized to make sure she understood.

"Why do you call me Little one? I mean, I know you're bigger than me—especially in your dragon form."

"The dragons that protect Wyvern are of a special breed. We take care of our mates completely. You could compare it to the Daddy Dom books you read."

She reacted strongly to his guess. "How do you know what I read? Can you read my mind?"

"Not unless you allow me into your thoughts, Ciel. We'll discuss that later." She looked very skeptical about that idea, but he continued, "I do not believe the mate bond would occur if your desires did not mesh completely with mine."

"You're a Daddy?" she whispered.

"Not a Daddy. Your Daddy."

# Chapter 5

Staring at him, Ciel struggled to figure out what to say or do. She'd become fascinated by that type of relationship in the last year when she'd found the first book. Instantly enthralled by the dynamics of a Daddy Dom and his Little, she'd devoured all the books she could find and had done her research.

As if her eyes opened for the first time, Ciel started noticing small things about couples around her. Her chemistry professor and his teaching assistant. Could they be? The way the quarterback of the football team fastened his girlfriend's seatbelt. Just control—or something else. Something more.

Her mind whirled inside her skull. Ciel could feel her head starting to hurt. She shook her head slightly, trying to fend it off.

"Stop thinking so hard, Ciel. We have a lifetime to figure everything out. You need water, food, and rest. The rest will wait. Okay?" he asked, with an expression that told her she didn't have another choice.

He was right. She was completely exhausted and over-whelmed. "Thank you." Ciel sagged against his strength.

"Come here, my Little Sky. Arms around my neck."

"Sky?" she asked before laughing at herself. "Because of my name. Ciel means sky in French. Do dragons speak French?"

"I've picked up a few things over the years." Argenis scooped her up in his arms and held her in place with one supporting arm as he grabbed her suitcase handle. "Tell me where your home is?"

Holding it together, she guided him through the old town to the second ring of houses. "There. That green door."

"It will have to be repainted," Argenis said arrogantly.

"Really? Why?"

"You belong to the silver dragon. Your family is now aligned with me."

"Is that silly?" she asked.

"Not at all," he answered before twisting the doorknob and walking inside as if the house belonged to him. After lifting the suitcase inside, he closed the door.

"Mom? I'm home," Ciel called.

"Ciel?" The thud of something heavy landing on the wooden table preceded the quick footsteps coming toward them.

In just a few seconds, her mother appeared. She paused for a moment at the sight of Ciel in the dragon's arms. "Are you hurt?"

"I ran into some barbed wire, and I didn't sleep on the way, but I'm okay. Argenis, you can let me down."

Slowly, he lowered her feet to the flooring. The protective dragon did not release her, but stood behind her so she could lean against his body. Looking over her shoulder, Ciel thanked him.

Her mother rushed forward to hug her, hesitating for a fraction of a second when Argenis didn't step back. "He didn't hurt you, did he?"

"No, Mom. Argenis has taken remarkable care of me. These scratches came from me freaking out when a dragon flew over me, changed into a person, and talked to me. Did you know there were dragons?"

"Your grandmother tried to tell me about them. I... Um... I thought she had dementia. Since meeting Argenis, I went through her papers and found a... A tome, I think you'd call it. And a bunch of pictures. Your great grandmother's sister was the mate of a dragon."

"Khadar, the emerald dragon," Argenis commented.

"I think that was his name," Ciel's mother said in surprise.

"You can look at the history later. Now, you need a shower and sleep. Where is your room?" he asked.

"I can take her there." Her mother tried to tug Ciel's arm.

"She is my mate. Have you read that section?" Argenis asked.

Ciel watched her mother's face and saw the answer. Whatever this tome was, her current condition was detailed inside. She looked back at Argenis to protest and snapped her mouth closed. He would not allow this now.

"I need to get caught up with sleep, Mom. And eat something other than peanut butter and jelly sandwiches."

"I can make you something on the grill. How about a hotdog and some veggies?" her mother suggested with a smile, knowing that was her favorite meal.

"With lots of mustard?"

"Of course. You go get cleaned up. I'll put a tray outside your room and knock when it's ready."

"Thank you, Mom. And thank you for getting help. I don't know that I would have made it home."

"You can tell me about it later. For now, push everything out of your head so you can rest." Her mother stepped forward to press a kiss to her cheek before disappearing back into the kitchen.

"Show me where your room is," Argenis directed, lifting her back into his arms.

"Down the hall. The second door on the left."

Ciel had never felt so completely devoid of energy. She couldn't even hold on to his neck. Somehow, he managed to get them and the suitcase through the doorway.

He sat her on the bed, and she closed her eyes. Able to track his movements with her hearing, she conserved energy. Ciel almost groaned aloud at the sound of the shower in the attached bathroom.

She dragged herself off the mattress and headed for the bathroom. Ciel pulled her torn and bloody T-shirt over her head as she walked. Strong hands gripped the material and pulled it off easily. "I can do it," she told Argenis.

"If I walk away, you will hurt with need and might drown in the shower. I'd promise to keep my eyes closed, but that won't happen. Let me unwrap my present," he coaxed, as he unfastened her jeans.

With sweeping caresses to her skin, Argenis smoothed her clothing, shoes, and socks off. The hungry look on his face told her he did not see all the flaws she did when she looked in the mirror. "Argenis?"

"Daddy."

"What?"

"It's time for you to call me Daddy."

He pulled his shirt over his head and pulled his belt from the loops on his pants. She froze as he wrapped the leather strip around his hand. "You're not going to spank me, right?" she blurted.

"Definitely. Now? No."

She opened her mouth to ask another question, but froze as he unzipped his pants and pushed them over his hips. In a few seconds, the most scrumptious collection of manly attractions appeared on a display she wouldn't forget. Ciel didn't know where to look. Maybe she'd start with those attractive V-shaped grooves at his hipbones.

Argenis stepped forward and lifted her chin up to close her mouth. "Ditto." Taking her hand, he led her into the shower.

The feel of the cool water was heavenly and distracted her for a moment. He pulled the clip, restraining her super-long tresses. She groaned with relief and allowed him to tilt her head back into the spray to wet her hair. Moving as if he was used to taking care of someone, Argenis turned her away from him before grabbing her shampoo and smoothing some on. A light floral scent filled the air as he gently coaxed the cleanser all the way to the ends of her hair.

Pretending not to feel the brush of his fingers on her hips, Ciel breathed a sigh of combined disappointment and relief when he finished. Those magical digits scratched her scalp lightly. "You can keep doing that forever."

"How about if I promise I'll wash your hair from now on?" he suggested.

"Deal," she agreed, as he tilted her head back into the water.

A few minutes later, she stood with conditioner in her hair as he squeezed a healthy amount of body wash into his hand. "I can wash myself."

"Not anymore."

She blinked at that statement as he smoothed the silky

cleanser over her skin. It felt so good to have the sweat and dirt of her struggle to make it home rinsed from her body. His hands didn't linger, but washed her completely.

Scooting away when he reached her pussy, Ciel knew what he would find. She was absolutely slick with her arousal. She couldn't help it. His touch, even on something as innocent as her shoulder or her face, did something to her inside.

He controlled her movements and slid his fingers into her wetness. "I would be very concerned if I didn't find you aroused."

"The mate bond," she whispered.

"Our bond, Little Sky. I want you equally hard." His hand left her pink folds to stroke over his hefty erection that she had tried to convince herself was an illusion. It wasn't.

As if unable to stop himself, Argenis pulled her close and kissed her deeply. Her arousal exploded. Ciel wrapped her arms around his neck and held on as he lifted her and carried her the short distance to press her against the tile at the side of the shower.

He ground his thick cock against her mound. Acting on instinct, she wrapped her legs around his waist. Argenis settled into her slick folds, drawing a moan from each of them.

A loud knock on the outer door interrupted.

"Mom," she whispered.

"She is taking care of you the best she can. She is also right. This isn't the time and place for me to claim my mate. Even if she is a heaven-sent temptress."

While Ciel celebrated his attraction to her, Argenis finished her shower quickly and rinsed the conditioner from her hair. When he'd bundled her in a towel with another one around her head, Argenis carried her back into the bedroom.

She inhaled two hotdogs, and some roasted vegetables before refusing a third.

"Then it is time for bed, Ciel. Where is your nightie?"

"I just wear a T-shirt."

"Little girls need pretty sleep things. We will rectify this," he promised as he swept the covers to the bottom of the bed. "For now, a soft shirt and Silly will do."

Ciel turned onto her tummy in the crisp sheets and pulled Silly close with one arm. Argenis settled behind her and towed her back a few inches until their bodies aligned.

"Night," she murmured, already half asleep.

"Sweet dreams, Little Sky."

# Chapter 6

He carried his mate over the threshold. A sense of rightness settled over him. Argenis could protect his mate anywhere, but having her in his lair satisfied the dragon inside him.

"This is your home?" she asked as soon as he'd set her feet on the beautiful wooden mosaic floor.

Watching her turn in a slow circle around in the foyer to appreciate all the treasures he'd collected over the years elated him. "This is my public space. My dragon's inner sanctum is much more protected."

"There are things in there that need to be safeguarded more? Is that a Van Gogh?" Ciel asked, walking toward the large painting that dominated the space.

"He was a tortured soul, but shared my love for the moon. He overindulged regularly in absinthe."

"Of course. That explains why you have a priceless painting in your foyer. Are you just rolling in money?"

"Are you asking to see my bank accounts?" he said with a smirk.

"No. I don't want to see them," she said, shaking her head

quickly. "Wait. Are you like an art dealer? How did you know Van Gogh drank absinthe?"

"I sat next to him at a bar one afternoon. The bartender knew him well and enjoyed gossiping. I settled his bar tab in exchange for the picture."

"You were at a bar with Van Gogh and paid his bill? How old are you?" she asked, looking so confused.

"I am as old as the mountains that surround Wyvern. Perhaps it's time we talked, now that you have rested."

"You think?"

"There are consequences for your actions, Ciel. Be careful. Let's go sit in the parlor."

He could hear her repeating the word parlor in a mutter under her breath. His mate delighted him.

"Now that we're in the *parlor*, tell me what's going on."

"This is the second time I'll warn you to not speak to me in that tone," Argenis warned, sending her a steely look that made her flop into a chair.

"Let me see if I can wrap history up in three sentences. Dragons rule. Your ancestors promised their daughters to the dragons who protect Wyvern. You are my mate."

"So, I'm your first mate?" she asked.

"No."

"I don't want to be part of a harem."

"A dragon only loves one woman at a time. His longevity helps lengthen his mate's life, but humans are fragile. When one mate dies, the dragon grieves their loss."

"But another mate is coming," Ciel insisted. "When I die, you'll just move on to the next."

"That is not correct. Do you think of Maureen's mother?"

"My grandmother? Of course. She was the sweetest. I loved to sit on her lap."

"Will you forget her with time?" Argenis probed.

"No. Are you saying you remember all your mates?"

"And treasure their memories," Argenis confirmed. "It is the curse of living a long time. You are forced to say goodbye to those you cherish."

"Tell me about your last mate."

"Everly was fifty when I found her. Her parents had moved away to another country when she was young. On a lark, she returned to visit where they had lived. When she drove through the mountain pass to enter Wyvern, I spotted her."

"How long were you together?" Ciel asked, leaning forward as if he'd captured her attention.

"At our first meeting, I knew she was ill. Dragons bring health to their mates. It is rare that any suffer from human diseases. Unfortunately, there was nothing that could be done. She would have lasted months if we had not met. As it was, we had five years together." Argenis reached up to wipe away the tear that streamed down his cheek.

Ciel stood and walked to his side. Her expression of exasperation disappeared and turned to concern. Argenis scooped her into his arms and sat her on his lap to hug his precious mate. Dragons learned quickly to focus on the now. The past held pleasant memories. The future? Unknown.

"That's really sad. Do you ever think having a mate isn't worth the habitual heartache?"

"No. Losing one makes me treasure the next even more."

He hugged her tight before sitting back slightly. "It also makes me establish rules to keep you happy and healthy."

"Rules? Like what? No running inside," she scoffed.

"If you wish to run, I will be glad to chase you outside," he suggested. "Dragons have a high predator instinct."

She stared at him with wide eyes for several seconds before whispering, "I just remembered I don't like to run."

"Smart," he said, knowing his smile was a bit dragonish. "You will follow my directions immediately, without question."

"That's harsh, don't you think?"

"No. You will allow me to care for you. A well-kept secret is that all mates identify as Little."

"Submissive?" she asked.

"Yes, but more specific. Little is spankier."

"Spankier?"

"A very good consequence for a mate."

"You're going to spank me if I don't follow your directions?" She looked at him as if he were crazy. Ciel wasn't able to control her expression completely. He could see the spark of sexual heat in her eyes and feel her body temperature rise.

"Yes."

"I don't think my ancestors agreed to that." She tried to dismiss the idea.

"Oh, they did. I'll be glad to show you in the contract."

That earned him a second look of disbelief.

"You rested and ate before we left your mother's house. Let me show you around our home."

Originally built to take advantage of the mountain breezes and natural light, Argenis's home was comfortable without the support of electricity. He led her through the main rooms and encouraged her to explore. Along the way, he introduced her to his staff. Everyone welcomed her warmly.

"Where does everyone live?"

"Some have relocated into the houses on my grounds. Others live in town. The groundskeeper collects everyone who doesn't wish to walk here, in a cart in the morning, and delivers them at home at the end of the day."

"People just moved here?"

"Yes. There were a few who lived outside the mountains ringing Wyvern. It is not safe there. I allowed their family to come here and found jobs for all," Argenis assured her as he walked past a heavily fortified metal door with old-fashioned locks along one side.

"What's in there?"

"My treasury. Dragons are collectors of all things precious. My wealth resides there."

"What if someone robs you?"

Argenis laughed and patted himself on the chest. "Dragon, remember?"

"That doesn't mean you're indestructible."

"Close. Let's worry about my demise on a different day. Here is our room," he said, waving her into the extensive suite.

Decorated in ice bluish-white colors with silver accents, it sparkled. Ciel walked inside and turned in a circle. "It's gorgeous. Did your last mate design it?"

He understood her true question. "This room, as well as many others in the house, is redesigned to welcome a new mate, no matter how long it takes for her to appear. I will change anything you wish. Your things have already been unpacked and Silly is in the adjoining room."

"Really? What's in there?"

She rushed forward to the door he'd nodded to, coming back to link her arm with his and drag him forward when the mate bond kicked in. "Come on."

He heard her gasp of shock when he opened the door. "What is this place?"

"It is your space. You can read, play games, nap, whatever you like," Argenis explained as he waved his hand toward different areas of the room.

"Does that say *naughty chair?*" she pointed to a wooden chair with no cushion facing the undecorated corner.

"Yes." He loved her shiver and knew she wasn't aware she had reacted so deliciously.

"I think it's time for your first spanking," he announced.

"What? Why? I didn't do anything bad."

"Come here, Little Sky." He walked into the room and guided her with a hand to her lower back to the big chaise lounge set up in her reading area. He sat on the long extension and drew her between his legs. Without explaining, he unfastened her jeans.

When she twisted away, he smacked her sharply on the bottom, shocking her into freezing in place. "This is a good girl spanking, but it can become more severe if you need it to be."

"Why are you taking off my pants?"

"Spankings require bare bottoms."

He had her jeans and panties lowered to her knees as she digested that fact. She didn't squirm again until he lifted her and draped her over his lap on her tummy. Her struggles were useless, but so very enjoyable.

Argenis held her in place easily and stripped off her shoes and the crumpled clothing around her ankles. Rubbing a hand over her bottom, he devoured the sight of her displayed over his thighs.

"Argenis, stop!"

"Daddy," he corrected her absentmindedly. "You can lie to yourself if you wish, Ciel, but never to me. I can smell your arousal." He traced the cleft of her bottom to her pussy, drawing her attention here. "How long have you wondered what a spanking would feel like?"

"Never! I never wondered that!"

"Careful, Little Sky. Dragons can also smell lies."

He swatted her lightly as a test. She froze in place for a split second before struggling to get away. Delivering a second firmer slap, Argenis was pleased to see her freeze and inhale deeply. That was it.

Keeping the impact at that level, he concentrated on bringing a uniform pink blush to her beautiful skin. Ciel continued to wiggle for a short time before her body relaxed and dangled. To reward her, Argenis delivered the next spank directly on the seam of her pussy.

"Ah!" she gasped, lifting her torso in reaction.

"You're alright, Ciel. Daddy knows all your secrets."

"Damn nose," she muttered.

"No cussing," he corrected her cheerfully as he moved her thigh to spread her legs. When she pulled them back together, he swatted her a bit firmer. "None of that. Back into position."

He continued to deliver harder strikes until she relented and followed his directions. "Good girl," he praised her and rewarded her with another light slap to her pussy. Her groan went straight to his cock, testing his control. She was completely wet.

Argenis altered light spanks with deepening caresses between her legs. Completely wet, Ciel's small whimpers and moans guided him in balancing pain and pleasure. When he heard a small sob, Argenis knew she'd reached the turning point to surrender to him.

"Daddy can't believe you're his, Ciel. Can you feel my cock pressing against your hip? You look absolutely ravishing stretched over my lap with a beautiful blush on your sweet bottom. Daddy's going to punish you often. Sometimes, he won't allow you to enjoy it. This time, I'm going to make you come so hard, you let him see the real Little girl inside you."

He traced around her drenched opening and pressed two

fingers deep inside. She was not a virgin, but not experienced. The silky walls of her tight passage clamped down on him. He couldn't wait to be buried deep inside her.

"I'm going to be here, Little Sky. Are you going to be brave and take me deep?" He scissored his fingers inside her to stretch her slightly. Giving her a slight bite of pain that he'd discovered she liked with pleasure.

She moved her head in a combination nod and shake that made him smile. Ciel was still trying to hide from him. He treasured her shyness. There would be so much to teach her to enjoy.

Brushing his thumb over her clit, Argenis watched her still and then gasp. Her body shook hard as her pleasure burst inside. He continued to stroke her until she hung limp over his lap.

"Come here, Ciel. Daddy needs to hold you."

He gathered her into his arms and rocked her slowly as he pressed his lips to her hair. "Precious mate. You please me."

"Argenis," she sighed.

"Daddy," he corrected.

"Daddy," she whispered.

"Good girl. That deserves another."

Her eyelids flew up, and she searched his face. He knew she was checking to see if he was joking. He leaned forward to capture her lips. Kissing her with all the surging passion inside him, Argenis showed her exactly what he thought of his mate.

As his mouth seduced hers, he slid his hand under her T-shirt. Rubbing his fingertips over one lace-covered breast, he loved how she lifted her ribcage to press herself closer. He rewarded that behavior with a light pinch to the beaded tip pressing against the lace.

Her delighted gasp made him deepen the kiss. He

stroked over her abdomen to glide over her soft mound. To his delight, she widened her thighs, allowing him greater access. Teasing her inner labia, Argenis memorized all the small sensitive spots that made her inhale sharply and repeatedly returned to push her arousal higher and higher.

"Daddy, I need you inside me."

"Soon, Little Sky. I'm going to fill you so full." He demonstrated, pushing two fingers back inside her body. Easing them out, he flicked his thumb over her clit lightly before repeating their entry faster.

Urgently straining against confinement, his cock felt like it would tear a hole in his pants. He wouldn't rush their union. He could wait until she was sure of her new reality.

He could feel the fluttering contractions of her inner walls and knew her orgasm was hovering. Releasing her lips, he leaned slightly to the side to whisper into her ear, "Now, Mate. Come now!" His bite to the curve where her neck and shoulder merged was the final stimulus she needed. With a cry, she came, clinging to him for support.

.

# Chapter 7

Ciel had trouble even looking at him. She'd never been so openly wanton in front of anyone—not that Argenis seemed bothered. He acted like spanking her butt and doling out orgasms was an everyday event. She'd had sex before, but like in bed... In the dark. Where he's naked, too.

She knew all his parts worked. They might work too well. The bulge in his pants looked ginormous. She felt herself becoming wet again. Stop!

It was like he had the magic key to ignite her arousal. Being close to him turned her on. Wandering too far made her crave him in a painful way. The sting from her punished bottom reminded her constantly of his demonstration of his control and her reaction to it.

Now at the end of the day, she sat on the patio on a lounge chair as he met with a few employees. It was unbelievable to think of everything they relied on for their normal lives. Now, everything had to be planned and organized.

The most able-bodied men and women had moved the cattle from the far pastures to those closer to the house that day. Those less mobile had organized a storage shed. They'd found the butter and cheese making tools. Another group excavated the mill and cleaned it to grind corn and wheat. Thanks to the longevity of the estate and Argenis's elaborate collections, they wouldn't starve and could help others in Wyvern.

A loud, bellowing sound made her jump to her feet. What was that?

"Come, Ciel," Argenis called, racing back to her side. He leaned close and scooped her up over his shoulder. Holding her close with a hand on her lower back, he ran for an open space.

"I don't like this. You'll have to come with me," Argenis told her as he set her feet on the grass. "Put that on!"

"What's happening?" she called back.

"Miss. The master would like you to wear this." The man who managed Argenis's holdings held up a thick leather jacket. "This will protect you," he explained as he helped her into it. "The silver dragon's skills are needed."

A whoosh of displaced air ruffled her hair. Automatically, she gathered it in her hands as she turned to see the magnificent creature a short distance away. He trumpeted and crooked his neck as if telling her to hurry.

Ciel thrust her long hair down inside the back of the jacket as she ran to him. Another loud call echoed through the sky, and she threw herself up onto his back. Argenis helped her, giving her a boost and stability as she scrambled on his scales. When she had settled into place, Ciel tightened her arms around his neck and yelled, "I'm ready."

She closed her eyes as he surged upward. Her hands tightened on his scales to hold on as securely as possible. This was like a reverse roller coaster, she thought to steady herself. Instead of the chug upward, this had the gravity rush that the downside of a monster coaster did. *Please don't let the down-ward ride be at supersonic speed.*

When they were level, his powerful wings impelled them through the air. She opened her eyes to see the most brilliant sunset. All the colors of yellow, orange, pink, and blue melting together took her breath away.

A flash of motion caught her eye. Jerking her head to the right, she almost lost her balance, but Argenis steadied her with a flex of his massive shoulders.

*Steady, Little Sky. This isn't the time to play catch.*

The deep raspy voice sounded inside her brain, startling her. Argenis. It could only be him.

Could she talk back to him? She thought really hard. *I'm okay.*

A huge bronze dragon took position next to Argenis. His jewel-like brown eye seemed to look right through Ciel. Mesmerized, she almost forgot to hold on, but caught herself as she swayed his way. She needed to stay away from that dragon, she decided.

Flames ahead drew her attention. She stretched upward to see better over Argenis's head. It was almost dark, but when the flames flared, she could see dark figures trying to get in through one of the mountain passes. Their covert actions made it clear they were not good guys.

*Close your eyes!*

Without hesitating, Ciel slammed her eyelids shut. Almost immediately a bright glow lit up the area around them. She squeezed her eyes closed harder as the light showed through her protective flesh. Shouts of anguish filtered up from the ground. Argenis flew pass after pass over the area until an eerie silence filled the air.

When the glow faded, Ciel dared to open her eyes. The scales on the dragon's neck were the first thing she saw. They glowed with an inner brightness that lessened as she watched. Looking at other parts of his body, she noted the same thing. Had that piercing light come from Argenis?

This time, when Argenis made a sweeping turn, he headed back toward his mountain. A thousand questions raced through her mind. Could all dragons emit light? What did it do? She looked behind her to see what had happened on the ground, but they were too far away.

She tried to think a message to Argenis, but errant thoughts kept zinging through her mind. Unable to focus, she could only wait until he was once again in human form to communicate. Whatever the threat had been, the dragons had repelled it.

The dragon landed with a resounding thud that almost unseated her. It was so totally different from when she'd ridden on his back before that Ciel slid down quickly and ran back to give him room. Almost instantly, he shifted in a dazzle of light.

"Argenis? Are you okay?" She rushed toward the man who had dropped to one knee—his posture bent toward the ground.

"I am okay, Little Sky. Just depleted."

"What can I do to help you?" she asked.

"Let's go inside. My staff will have everything I need."

Ciel wrapped her arm around his waist when he stood to support him. She could tell he was operating on sheer willpower as he moved mechanically. That athletic, smooth pace that normally characterized his walk had vanished.

He headed inside and directly to the kitchen. A feast was laid out on the candle-lit kitchen table. Argenis took a seat and began inhaling food.

"Eat, Ciel, if you are hungry," he instructed.

She helped herself to a piece of cheese and a cracker to

nibble on as she looked around the darkened kitchen. "I've never been in here."

"This is my staff's space. They eat here together often. We have all become a family."

"What happened out there?"

"My apologies, Little one. Due to the mate bond, I couldn't leave you here. I would never put you at risk," he assured her.

"I wasn't worried about me. I figured it was an emergency. What were those people doing?"

"People are becoming desperate. Food is becoming scarcer as everything in freezers starts to rot. That was a raiding party. They thought by breaking through the barriers at night, we would not be able to respond."

"So... You made it... not night?" she suggested hesitantly, trying to figure this out as she talked.

"Correct."

"So, you're like a giant nightlight?" Ciel asked.

A bark of laughter erupted from his throat at that visual image. "Ciel, you delight me. Yes. That is exactly what I am."

"Do all dragons glow?"

"No. The power of the moon belongs only to silver dragons," he explained as he devoured his third sandwich.

"Does everyone else have a power?" she asked, completely enthralled.

"Dragons are the definition of power," he told her in a tone somewhere between proud and simply factual.

Surprised that she understood that statement completely, Ciel nodded as she helped herself to a piece of the freshly baked bread. She froze when he took it from her. Ciel watched him slather butter over the top of it.

"Try this," he suggested as he handed it back.

"Thank you," she said, relaxing. Even famished, he

focused on taking care of her. Taking a big bite, she wiggled happily in her chair at the delicious flavor.

"Are you going to be okay?" she asked a few minutes later, amazed as he depleted the volume of food left for him.

"I'm already fine, Little Sky. Normally, I would have feasted on a cow to replenish myself. I didn't think you needed to see that," he said with a smirk.

"Oh!" A visual image popped into her mind.

"Exactly."

"I heard you in my mind," she whispered, to change the subject.

"Yes. When you're ready, we can make that easier," he commented casually.

"How? Why do I have to be ready?" she asked, confused.

"It involves opening the barrier in your mind between us."

"I don't understand," she said, shaking her head.

He scooted his chair back and plucked Ciel up to sit her on his lap. "I want to hold you for this, Little one. Close your eyes, Ciel."

When she followed his directions, he pressed a hand to her forehead. "Concentrate on the front of your mind. When you're ready, turn around to face everything behind you."

When she turned physically, he prevented her movement. "I'm sorry, Ciel. I didn't explain that well. You're going to do everything in your mind. Imagine you're following my directions and it will happen—inside."

"Oh. Sorry."

He leaned forward to kiss her forehead before leaning back. "Close your eyes and focus on that kiss."

Obediently, she followed his instructions.

"Now, in your mind, turn to look at everything behind you."

"Wow!" She couldn't look at everything at the same time. Lights flashed from all directions. It was so beautiful.

"Do you see a silver light?" he asked.

"Silver like you?" she blurted.

"Yes, Little Sky."

"There it is."

"Focus on that one. Follow its path through your mind. It will weave around many other colors. Don't lose your focus. It is easy to become confused."

She sensed that would be bad. Laser focusing her attention down to the silvery light, she traced it to where it ended at a barrier. "I found the end. It disappears behind a door with a three locks. One is already open."

"That happened when we met. Reach out and press your hand to the door, leaving your print on it. Remember how you got here. In an emergency, you can open all the locks, connecting our minds. Never open any other door for your safety."

"Okay," she said and heard her voice quake.

"If you're ready to connect us further, open the second one. Be prepared," he warned as she turned the deadbolt.

A rush of sensations streamed toward her. Startled, she opened her eyes to find herself gazing directly into his eyes. "Argenis?"

"Daddy. Try talking to me in your mind."

*Argenis?*

*Daddy.*

*I didn't have to shout that time.*

*Our connection is closer now.*

Pulling her gaze from his, Ciel laid her head on his broad shoulder. All the changes that had happened in the last few days boggled her mind. How could everything turn upside down in such a short time? Not just the lack of technology, but the transformation inside her. His soft kiss on her hair drew her from her thoughts.

*Daddy?*

*Yes, Ciel.*

*Is this real?*

"Yes, Little Sky. Is life with me so difficult?" he teased aloud. His voice sounded loud in the quiet house, making her jump.

"No. I could have never envisioned all this happening, but... It feels right."

"That is the best indicator that we are on the right path." He rubbed her back with one hand as he reached for a handful of walnuts. Popping a few in his mouth, he rocked her gently as she struggled to address everything brewing inside her.

"The dragons will continue to protect Wyvern?" she asked, still slightly frightened by the events of the evening.

"To our last breaths. Our oath was not easily given for that exact reason. We made a promise to keep Wyvern safe."

"Thank you for keeping my family safe."

"Your family is mine now."

After another minute, he told her, "I am finished. Is there anything else you would like?"

"Like that one piece of cheese?" she joked, pointing to one of the last items that had welcomed them home.

He reached forward and plucked the slice from the board it sat on. Bringing it close to her mouth, he tempted her as if he fed her. When she opened her mouth, he quickly placed the bite into his mouth.

"Hey! That was mine."

"You wouldn't begrudge an old, tired dragon a small slice of cheese. Would you?" he teased as he stood easily, lifting her into his arms.

"I can walk, Argenis. You should conserve your energy."

"Good idea." He shifted her to drape over his shoulder. One large hand swatted her bottom, reigniting the heat from her spanking. "This is totally not taxing."

She tried not to look at his firm butt as she bounced with every step he took. That was an impossible task. What she wanted to do was grab a handful and squeeze.

*Gently, please.*

The polite request echoed through her skull as he neared their bedroom. "You can read my thoughts?" she squeaked.

"Only the stressed or aroused ones."

Her mind whirled as she digested that. "Maybe unlocking that door wasn't a good idea."

"It works both ways, Little Sky," he shared as he lowered his torso to set her gently on the bed. "Sleep now. Then I'll show you."

# Chapter 8

*I can read his thoughts when he's aroused?*

Ciel ignored the stressed part as he stripped off her clothing and ushered her into the shower. Did dragons suffer from anxiety? They could just flame anything that got in their way.

She could tell his strength was returning as time passed, but she could still see the lines of exhaustion on his face. Reaching for the soap, she eyed the expanse of his broad shoulders as he dipped his head under the water. Laying her hands on him gently, Ciel massaged and washed his back.

"That feels good, Ciel," he said with a groan.

Loving the feel of his hard muscles under the silky cleanser, she enjoyed helping him relax. *While copping a feel.* Ciel smothered the laugh that threatened to burst from her lips at this thought. She dared to smooth the soap over his taut buttocks and heard his groan change from enjoyment to something more.

"Turn around, Daddy," she requested.

When he turned around, she discovered just how much her touch had pleased him. Pretending to ignore his jutting cock, Ciel repeated her care on his chest and torso. Her fingers brushed the thick shaft as she lathered his stomach. Reaching his pelvis, she dared to try to wrap her fingers around his shaft and pull gently from root to tip.

The resulting roar that erupted from his mouth didn't scare her in the least. She rose onto her tiptoes and pressed a kiss to his lips as she continued to stroke his sensitive flesh.

Argenis raised a hand to tangle in her long hair at the base of her skull. He held her securely in place as he took control of the kiss. The desire that seemed to brew constantly inside her flared hotter as he explored her mouth with such sensuality that it made her ache for more. She ground herself against his thickness when her hands were trapped between their bodies.

"Mate, I can wait no longer," he growled a few seconds later when he released her mouth.

"Please. I need you."

He turned her body into the spray to rinse off the lather that had transferred to her skin. Ciel could feel the sharp streams of water more than ever before. He smoothed his hands over her skin. Cupping her breasts, he squeezed them lightly before rolling the tight nipples.

"You are so beautiful, Ciel. I am a very lucky dragon."

"Make love to me," she whispered.

"My pleasure, Little Sky."

He quickly rinsed the lather from his body before toweling most of the moisture from their skin with rough, urgent strokes. She loved that he wanted her as much as she craved his touch. Ciel looped her arms around his shoulders as he carried her to the gigantic bed.

After ripping the covers from the beautifully made bed and sending pillows flying across the room, he placed her gently in the middle of the bed as he stretched out beside her. Ciel turned immediately to face him, but Argenis leaned forward to press her onto her back as he captured her lips in a steamy kiss that made her cling to him for stability.

His hand roamed over her body. She loved his caresses. Argenis seemed to know exactly where she needed to be touched and kissed. Her arousal growing, she ground herself against his powerful thigh inserted between hers. She knew he could feel her wetness and didn't care. The feeling swirling inside Ciel erased her self-consciousness.

Craving his touch on her breasts, Ciel cupped herself to draw his attention. He froze, watching her hands move on her own body.

"Damn! That's sexy," he told her in a low tone that sent shivers down her spine. "My turn."

Stroking his hands up her sides, he brushed her hands away to take over. His touch felt totally different. The tips of his fingers were rough against her skin, making each caress more captivating. The thrill of his hands holding her and exploring her body rocked Ciel. She'd never felt so sensitive.

The scratch of his soft beard against her skin added a dimension of touch. He kissed the spot behind her ear and she shivered as a zing went through her whole body. *How does he know what will drive me crazy?*

Ciel loved the feel of his skin. There was something different about it. An image of Argenis in dragon form burst into her head. Those glowing scales that reflected the light, seeming hard and warm simultaneously. She didn't know how that could be sexy, but it was. He was sex personified.

When he shifted over her, she wrapped her hands around his broad shoulders, afraid he would move away or stop. "Please," she whispered. "I need you."

"Mine," he growled with a fierce expression that told her

he would fight to the death to keep her. His possessiveness sent a thrill through her.

"Yours," she agreed. "And you're mine."

He kissed her hard before shifting to settle on his knees between her parted legs. She watched him scan her body slowly as she posed in front of him. His glance felt almost as real as a touch. She watched his expression become hungrier —if that were even possible. Never had she felt this wanted.

Staring at her, Argenis slid a hand down his chiseled torso and over one of his thick thighs. He cupped his balls and tugged on them slightly before releasing himself. She couldn't tear her gaze away as he moved his fingers upward. The sight of his hand moving on his own body was so erotic. She could feel her juices gush from her as he roughly gripped his thick shaft.

His fist closed around the steely erection, lowering it to fit his cock against her entrance. The feel of the wide head pressing into her was intimidating. He was definitely blessed with girth and length. With a slow, controlled thrust, he glided inside, aided by her slick juices. The feel of him brushing against every tiny space inside her was shiver-worthy. She'd never known sex could feel this good.

As he moved deeper inside her, suddenly, it was too much. She bit her lip as she felt her body struggling to stretch around him—her inner panic making it worse. He smoothed a finger over her mouth, drawing her attention there, before leaning down to kiss her fiercely. As she threaded her fingers through his hair, he lifted her right leg to wrap it around his waist. Instantly, the pressure eased to a level that thrilled her once again. She felt herself relaxing around him.

"Good girl," he whispered against her lips before leaving a trail of kisses down her neck as he lowered himself toward her body. Supporting his mass on one forearm, Argenis allowed her to feel a bit of his weight, pinning her in place. He was in charge. There was no doubting that.

Moving his free hand, he traced a path over her shoulder and across her collarbone as he continued to push forward into her tight pussy. She held her breath when his path led down the center of her body. He paused between her breasts before trailing his fingertips over one puckered peak. His path didn't hesitate there but moved over the sensitive underside. He drew a zigzagging pattern drawn on her skin, brushing his thumb across her delicate mound. In a stunning burst of sensations, he bit her shoulder as he pinched her nipple and thrust the last small distance inside her.

She clamped her hands around his shoulders as she inhaled sharply. He held himself deep inside her, allowing Ciel to adjust to his size. A sharp need built inside her. She needed more.

"Move!" she demanded.

He chuckled softly and withdrew slowly, stroking across sensitive spots in reverse as effectively as he'd passed them before and firing up new sizzling points she had no idea even existed. What else could he surprise her with? She pressed a kiss to his chest to encourage him.

Argenis slid a hand under her hips and lifted her slightly. He thrust back inside her, watching her face. Withdrawing, he adjusted his angle slightly and pushed forward again. This time she gasped, "There."

His movements sped up as he drove her quickly toward her climax. She clung to him, pressing kisses to his skin. The air heated around them. Ciel loved the salty taste of the moisture that built on his skin as they moved together. When he ground the root of his cock against her that was the last push she needed.

As her body clamped around him, Argenis quickened his

movements. With a roar, he emptied himself inside her. That dragon symbol on her hand heated and glowed silver. Suddenly, she could feel his pleasure. The sensation of her velvety walls milking his shaft.

Overwhelmed by the blending of their climaxes, she felt her orgasm strengthen and grow. "Daddy!" she screamed into the room as his roar resounded on the walls.

When their heart rates had settled slightly, he gathered her to his chest and rolled onto his back. Feeling boneless, she draped himself over his strength. Her eyes closed in contentment. As she drifted to sleep, she felt him kiss her hair.

"Mate," he growled. "Mine."

"Yours," she mumbled in agreement.

# Chapter 9

Watching Ciel wave goodbye to him from the ground always tore his heart apart. Now that the mating was complete, he could join the other dragons alone in their forays against those who would attack Wyvern. Today, he was on a mission to find a piece for the mill.

The grinding stone had become chipped over the years. The man who had maintained and run the mill as a historical site had talked to a supplier three towns away many months ago. Argenis would fly to contact the man and transport the replacement if it still existed.

It might be a fool's errand or possibly keep the town able to produce substantial amounts of milled flour for years to come. In the old days, a dragon would escort a group going by wagon. Unfortunately, the camps outside Wyvern had grown desperate as food stocks dwindled.

The town was allowing some to enter if they seemed safe —families with willing workers. The militia groups of men were repelled each time they attempted to breach a barrier. In the beginning, many chose to attack at night. That quickly became their last choice when faced with a dragon who lit up the ground and eliminated any threat. Now, they lay in wait, looking for a good opportunity.

Winging his way over the mountain range, Argenis roared a massive burst of fire. Angry settlers often chose to launch weapons toward the dragons as they left the area. Fire forced them back and discouraged any hostilities. He paused to note any threats. It appeared that the raiding forces had lessened. Perhaps they were moving on.

Pleased that all the citizens would be safer, including his mate, Argenis forged ahead with massive thrusts of his powerful wings. Quickly, he covered the distance, looking for the landmarks the miller had shared. A red flag caught his eye. He swooped in to land in a small clearing. Changing, he discovered an audience observed him from the nearby buildings.

The small group did nothing to appear dangerous. He waved and strode toward the man that emerged to greet him. "Are you Jenkins? Samuel, the miller at Wyvern sent me."

"I am. I'll admit you're the first dragon I've had land in my yard. My kids may never be the same."

Argenis couldn't help but grin. "I should have set something on fire."

"I have a trash pile you could ignite for us if you like," he commented before adding, "I bet there's something you're here for."

"Is the grinding wheel still available?" Argenis asked.

"It's laying over in the field there. No one can move it now." He looked at the man he'd seen land and transform. "I'm guessing you could handle it. I can't just give it to you," he warned.

"What do you need?" Argenis asked.

"Our medicine supplies are dwindling. Would you be willing to try a pharmacy or two for us?" the miller asked.

"Give me a list and I'll do my best. I can't guarantee that I can find anything," Argenis said.

"Thank you."

A woman rushed out of the shadows with a fussy infant on her shoulder. "Thank you, sir. The baby... She's always needed medicine. It wasn't a problem before, but now..." Her voice trailed off and Argenis could hear the concern.

"I'll do my best. Write down anything you think I'll need to know," Argenis requested.

"What's happening out there?" the miller asked.

"It's not good. Are you safe here?" Argenis asked.

"We're not sure. From the beginning, I've invited neighbors to gather here on my land to support each other. So far, no one has made it here. I don't know if they've changed their minds or..." The miller shook his head, obviously suspecting the worst had happened.

"Would you be interested in coming to Wyvern? I can call for another dragon to carry your family to safety."

"I hate to leave my mill. People need someone here who knows how to work it."

"We can talk when I return. Discuss it with your family."

"Thank you. What is your name?"

"Argenis."

"Thank you, Argenis," Jenkins said with honest gratitude.

A few seconds later, his wife reappeared with a short list. "We tried to get this from the pharmacy in town, but a group of thugs has taken it over. They'd let us exchange flour for a while. Now, they want something different." Her eyes drifted meaningfully to her stunning teenage daughter.

"I will be back. I've offered to take your family to Wyvern. Eventually, they will travel here to collect anything they want," Argenis warned.

"I didn't want to leave the medicine I knew the pharmacist had ordered for the baby. If we have that, we should leave," she agreed.

"Gather whatever is most essential and what could help those in Wyvern. They will welcome you."

She nodded and turned to scurry back into the house, taking the children in with her.

"I will gather all the parts from the mill and my tools. Those will be needed," Jenkins suggested.

"Put them in a sturdy container that I can lift with a claw," Argenis requested.

"Weight restrictions?"

"You won't need to worry about that."

Turning, Argenis returned to the clearing and tucked the note safely into his pocket. It would be there when he shifted back to human. In a flash of light, he resumed his dragon form and took to the sky.

The pharmacy was close. In the middle of a shopping area, it and the grocery store next door were now barricaded with debris piled on cars. Argenis swooped down to bash one section away with a flick of his hind leg. It was more effective than he'd imagined as a fourth of the circle went flying across the parking lot.

Men rushed from the building to look up at the sky. They fired guns after him, making Argenis skyrocket upward out of the way. Several bullets bounced off his scales and one grazed his snout. The sting made Argenis snort.

*Are you okay?*

*I am fine, Little Sky. I will be home soon.*

Argenis smiled slightly in a dragon grimace at her concern. Their connection was strong.

Turning his attention back to the men below, Argenis released his light. He watched the men shield their eyes, fall to their knees, and collapse, dropping the guns to the ground.

He landed and sent another burst of pure white to address anyone inside who had not shot at him.

A quick shift and he cautiously dashed inside. That second indirect blast had knocked out the resistance. They'd wake up with headaches but would be totally functional in a few days.

Argenis strode through the pharmacy, noting all the things inside that could help others. He shook his head at the thought of men profiting from the needs of others during this tough time. Searching through the stacks of medicine, he found the remainder of a large canister holding the medicine Jenkins needed. He took it and checked off the other items. Perusing the drugs that remained on the shelves, he grabbed a container of a well-known antibiotic and a supply of bandages. After stuffing everything into a backpack from the shelf, he left the rest for others who would need help.

"Can I go in there?" A woman stood just outside the entrance as if scared to go in. "My father..."

Argenis spoke when she hesitated. "It is safe inside. Gather what you absolutely need and pass the word to others. The men inside won't wake up for twenty-four hours."

"Thank you!" She rushed inside and returned with several vials and syringes. As she ran down the street, she announced, "The pharmacy is open for a day. Go now. Get only the essentials!"

Argenis shifted, and after grabbing the bundle of supplies, took to the sky. From above, he could see people emerging from different buildings to race toward the freed complex. Hopefully, a new crew would not replace the old.

# Chapter 10

"You're hurt!" Ciel reached to touch the welt on Argenis's nose.

"It is nothing and will soon disappear," he promised. "The new grinding stone is being installed as we talk."

"They shot at you?"

"Not the miller and his family. For their safety, I brought them here to Wyvern," Argenis tried to distract her. "Keres came to help."

"The black dragon. He's scary."

"When did you meet Keres?" Argenis asked. She could tell he was concerned by the furrow on his brow.

"He came here after you left."

"Send a message to me immediately if he shows again," Argenis ordered.

"O—okay. Is he dangerous?"

"I don't believe so," Argenis answered slowly as he was considering his words carefully. "Now, someone is coming to meet you."

"Who?"

"The gold dragon, Drake, and his mate. Her name is Aurora."

"What a pretty name! I think I remember someone named Aurora in school. She was a few years older than me, I think," Ciel suggested.

"I think you're right. She just finished college."

"When are they coming?" Ciel asked, lifting a hand to smooth over her hair. She had given up putting on make-up and there were no blow dryers or curling irons. Her split ends were out of control, but there was no way she could cut the long tresses herself.

"I see them now."

Ciel turned and raced back into the house. The cool shadows of the house slid over her heated skin as she ran for the bathroom. After quickly washing her face and putting a bit of powder on, Ciel brushed her hair and started braiding it into a thick plait.

*Come.*

She raced back through the house as she finished weaving her hair together. As she walked out the door, Ciel spotted the gold dragon shimmer into an amazingly fit man. A woman stood with her back to the house.

"Hi," Ciel called as she finished the braid and wrapped a scrunchie around it.

"Ciel. I thought that name was familiar. I think we were in physical education together in high school," Aurora said with a smile.

"I recognized your name, too. I'm sorry I don't remember better. Freshman year was the absolute worst," Ciel confessed.

"No problem. I'm glad to meet you now. Let me introduce my mate, Drake."

"Hi, Drake," Ciel said with a wave.

"I am glad to meet you, Ciel. Congratulations on your mating," Drake told her in a voice even deeper than Argenis's.

"Ciel, I am going to show Drake something on the map while he's here. Why don't you show Aurora the swings in the back?" Argenis suggested.

"That sounds like fun," Aurora beamed.

"Come on. Argenis just put them up for me," Ciel said, waving to Aurora to follow her.

The two settled in the simple swings made with smooth wood and ropes. Pushing off with their legs, they swung back and forth for a while. Finally, Ciel asked, "Had you heard of the dragons?"

"My grandmother was the keeper of information for my family. She had not talked to me yet. I was clueless. I met Drake as he was going into the cemetery for his former mate's burial," Aurora shared.

"His mate had just died?" Ciel asked, horrified.

"Yes. How long ago did Argenis's mate pass? I'd heard she was sick."

"I—I don't know how long. I know he loved her. That's hard to know that the person you love has felt so strongly for other women." Ciel looked at the woman she knew understood. "Does that bother you?"

"It did in the beginning. Then I realized I didn't want Drake alone for centuries."

"I didn't think about it like that. That helps. Thank you," Ciel expressed her genuine gratitude.

"I'm glad to meet another person who just mated with a dragon. How does he treat you?" Aurora asked.

Ciel could tell there was a purpose for her question. She was asking for information. "It's great, unless I get spanked," she blurted, hoping that she wasn't making a major blunder.

"Oh, thank goodness. I wondered if it was just Drake and me." She paused and smiled at Ciel. "It's like all my fantasies have come to life."

"Do you think they're all Daddies? I mean... Is Drake a Daddy Dom?" Ciel dared to ask.

"The Daddiest. He takes very good care of me."

Noting the slight blush on her new friend's face, Ciel said, "Could they be any hunkier? Are there any wimpy dragons?"

"I doubt that. I think it's part of their dragon shifter DNA. They're powerful in both forms. It fascinates me to watch Drake shift. It's like magic."

"I know. How can it possibly work? Where do their clothes go? And all the scales?" Ciel asked, laughing.

Aurora snickered. When their gazes met, peals of laughter bubbled from their lips. Instantly, they were the best of friends. All of Ciel's hesitations to reveal her new lifestyle evaporated.

"I'm glad you came," Ciel told her.

"Me, too. Drake didn't give me a choice," Aurora admitted.

"Want to come see my playroom?" Ciel asked.

"I'd love to."

"Come on. It's off our bedroom."

Ciel led the way into the house. They passed Drake and Argenis in his study, cut crystal glasses of an amber liquid in their hands. When they were safely passed, she whispered, "I thought they were looking at a map."

"We had to locate where the scotch came from, Little Sky," Argenis called after them. "Have fun!"

"Thanks, Daddy," Ciel automatically answered, a bit shocked that he had heard her. The moment the second word left her lips, she whirled to look at Aurora in shock. "I mean..."

Aurora interrupted her. "We're going to Ciel's playroom, Daddy."

"Be good, Little girl," Drake's low voice reverberated down the hallway.

Taking her friend's hand, Ciel dragged her into the playroom, where she hoped the men couldn't hear her. "Thank goodness you call Drake Daddy, too. I thought you'd laugh at me."

"Of course not. A—you're my friend. B—Daddy Dom, what else are we going to call them? C—Drake insists."

"Argenis does, too. I like it," Ciel confessed.

"Me, too. He takes really good care of me," Aurora said, waggling her eyebrows meaningfully.

"You are so bad," Ciel accused with a giggle.

A few minutes later, they'd chosen a board game and were happily rolling dice and moving pieces around. It was the perfect fun to have as they compared their lives and found so many similarities.

"I don't suppose we can play," Argenis asked from the doorway.

"Of course, Daddy. Come join us. You can have the gray marker and Drake can have the orange one. We'll pretend they're silver and gold," Ciel promised.

"Deal. Prepare to go down," Argenis challenged Drake.

"Bring it on."

The women looked back and forth between the two before dissolving into laughter. Their peaceful game had just taken on a totally new tone. Aurora looked at Ciel and winked. Immediately, Ciel understood. They were going to work together to make sure one of them won.

Ciel picked up the dice and rolled. "Oh, sorry, Daddy. You get to go back two spaces."

"I haven't moved yet," he pointed out.

"According to the rules, that means you miss your next turn," Aurora volunteered.

"Indeed? Well, I'll just occupy myself while I wait to play." Argenis plucked Ciel off the carpet and plopped her gently on his lap. He rubbed her back with his fingertips, massaging her.

Ciel couldn't keep her eyes from lowering to half-mast. "Maybe we should ignore that rule."

Even through lowered eyelids, Ciel saw Drake looking at his mate speculatively. Aurora must have noticed, too.

"Who likes that silly rule? Go ahead and take your turn," Aurora suggested.

"Thank you," Argenis said graciously. He kissed Ciel's hair and sat her back in her original spot before picking up the dice and rolling.

The women just looked at each other. Who could win against cunning dragons?

# Chapter 11

While Argenis was occupied himself with protection duty, Ciel pored over the thick tome that her grandmother had safeguarded during her lifetime. She wished she'd had a clue about the dragons. Who knew they lived in the mountains surrounding Wyvern? It definitely wasn't anything she remembered people talking about. The large stone sculpture in the square should have made her think, but she'd just loved climbing on it as a child.

Now as an adult, she read the history of Wyvern and was mind-boggled. The meeting between the settlers and the dragons must have terrified the town folk. Those brave men and women had kept everyone safe.

She wondered if they'd believed that the dragons would care for their mates as they'd signed it. Were they just protecting the majority at the cost of a few? Ciel found a few statements in the pact that showed they were not sacrificing their offspring. They believed the dragons' promise to take only those who were mates. Those they swore to protect with their life's blood.

Reading the story of the first mate fascinated her. Zinnia had received the first mark as the Black Dragon, Keres, had exited that meeting. Her hat blew off as he walked by. When he returned it, their hands touched, resulting in the searing dragon pattern. Her life as a treasured mate was briefly detailed, as well as her death at one hundred and thirty-seven.

Ciel couldn't imagine living that long. Then she thought of Argenis. Suddenly, all those years were very desirable. Even with the hardships of no technology, life with Argenis was a delight.

"Trying to find the skeletons in my closet?" a deep voice asked from behind her.

Jumping automatically from the surprise, Ciel whirled around to see Argenis leaning against the wall. "Daddy!"

Argenis caught her when she dashed to him and jumped into his arms. "Whoa, Little Sky. What if I'd dropped you?"

"That would never happen," she answered confidently.

"I'm glad you trust me, Ciel."

She nodded before tilting her head to look at him quizzically. "What are you doing here?"

"I'm heading out to do a survey of the path to the ocean. Want to go?"

"That's hundreds of miles away. How long will it take to get there?"

"Dragon," he answered simply, and tapped himself on the chest.

"How could I forget that?" she answered, laughing.

"Go get your swimsuit and let's go."

In a flash, she quickly abandoned her study of the old tome and dashed down the hall to their bedroom. Returning in a flash, Ciel had her bikini in her hand. A strap swung free as she hurried.

"Do we need a towel?" Ciel asked, trying to think where a beach towel would be in the house.

"Dragon," Argenis reminded her and then blew a draft of warm air over her body.

"Ooh! I like having my own personal towel boy?" she said with a grin.

"It's a long way down when we're up in the air, Little Sky," he glowered at her.

"You won't drop me."

"You sound pretty confident about that."

"I am."

"Come on, Miss Confident."

He ushered her out of the house, muttering "towel boy" under his breath. In the clearing out front, Argenis changed into dragon form and lowered his head for her to climb up on his neck.

Instead of moving into position quickly, Ciel took time to kiss his snout. "Thank you."

He blew a puff of smoke that made her rock back on her heels. As she watched, the white haze formed into a perfect heart and floated away.

"Do it again," she begged.

*Your swim time is getting shorter and shorter.*

"Okay. I'll get on, but only if you'll puff a heart for me later," she requested as she stuffed her bathing suit down the back of her tucked-in shirt to free her hands.

*Deal.*

In a short time, they were soaring through the clouds. So high that Ciel couldn't see what was happening down below with any real clarity. The air was gusty, so she put her face down to press against him. The slow, rhythmic beat of his wings flexed the muscles under her body, almost rocking her.

She jerked herself awake a few times when she caught herself drowsing.

*Sleep, Little Sky. I'll keep you safe.*

*And wake me up if anything exciting happens?*

*Of course.*

Ciel awoke as the hard surface below her changed its angle to descend. *Are we there yet?* She laughed.

*Almost, Little Sky. Can you see the dolphins playing in the water?*

*Oh! There's the ocean.*

Her family had visited the seaside one summer. She'd enjoyed it tremendously. Probably more than anyone else in her family. Ciel watched the waves crash on the beach. Other than a small cluster of fishermen, the strip of sand was uninhabited.

*No one has time for a vacation.*

*The world has changed, Little one. We will take time to enjoy the beach and then we'll accomplish our task.*

*What's that?*

*Something for your Daddy to take care of, Ciel.*

Ciel scrunched her mouth up at that response. She liked to know what was going on. *Daddy could tell me and then I wouldn't have to worry about it while I'm enjoying the beach.*

*Be good.*

Shutting her mouth with a snap, Ciel stopped asking questions. It must be something important. She still wondered why she couldn't know what it was, but her bottom knew it was wise not to argue with Argenis. She'd never win.

When he slowed, she tightened her grip on his scales. That was totally unnecessary as he landed with an easy thump. Ciel scrambled off his back and gave him some space to change.

Her jaw dropped in surprise when he lumbered past her

in dragon form to wade into the water. Ciel ran after him, hesitating at the edge. "Daddy? Do dragons swim?"

*Of course, Little Ciel. I like water a lot. Not as much as the Green Dragon. He's closely aligned with nature and loves to wallow in rivers and lakes.*

She continued to talk to him aloud. It seemed more normal to her when he could hear her. "Do you float or sink?"

He moved a bit further out into the water and disappeared. Ciel watched the surface and saw him show up a few feet away. She waded in a bit more, wanting to get in and play with him. Turning, she looked for a sheltered place to change.

When she shifted back to look toward the ocean, she jumped in surprise to see his dragon head a foot from her. "You scared me. How can you move that quietly?"

*Dragon.*

"Of course. That explains everything," she said, lifting her hands out in an exasperated motion.

His chuckle resounded in her head as he moved. Curving his body into a U-shape, Argenis provided a guarded area around her. She could only see the ocean in front of them. Quickly, she stripped off her clothes and slipped into her bikini while under the watchful silver eye of her mate.

"I'm ready."

Argenis scanned her outfit. *That's almost like wearing nothing.*

"I don't think anyone will come flirt with me while I have a dragon guardian."

*Daddy.*

"Yes, Daddy." She accepted his correction without hesitation. "Can we go swimming now?"

When he nodded toward the water, she knew he was waiting for her to lead the way. Turning, she darted toward the ocean and raced forward. "It's freezing!" she yelled over her shoulder, refusing to stop until she reached a point where the water covered her beaded nipples. She knew she'd never adjust to the temperature of the water until her sensitive peaks were under the surface. "Damn, that's cold."

*No cussing.*

"You don't think it's cold?"

*Come stand by me.*

As she moved closer, Ciel felt the water becoming warmer. He was like a water heater. She sidled up next to him to enjoy the heat radiating from him. "Mmm!"

With a snap of his tail, Argenis flicked water on her, soaking her completely.

Grateful she wore her hair in a braid, Ciel flipped the soaked plait over her shoulder and wiped the straggling hairs from her face. When she could see, she calmly swam away from him, kicking water to pay him back. Sure that she had doused him, Ciel peeked over her shoulder and found him enjoying the shower like it was a multi-head shower massager.

Shaking her head at her failed attempt to pay him back, Ciel let her feet sink back to the sand. Eep! She disappeared under the surface of the water. She'd reached the sudden drop-off of the land and was way over her head.

Argenis was there immediately to lift her up to the surface with a supporting tail. *Little Sky.*

"I wasn't expecting that," she sputtered.

*Indeed.*

"Are you laughing at me?"

*No. Never.*

She could hear the suppressed laughter bouncing around in his mind. It was impossible to resist his amusement. She had to laugh at herself.

*Want to do some exploration?*
"Like snorkeling?"
*You'll have to hold your breath.*
"I'm good at that," Ciel assured him.
*Climb onto my back and let's go.*

# Chapter 12

Moving slowly to not jostle his mate, Argenis forged through the water along the beach. The small pile of clothes Ciel had left on the sand waited patiently for him. Their explorations and the sunshine had sapped Ciel's energy. His mate was almost asleep on his back.

Watching her reaction to the various sea creatures they'd encountered had pleased him to the core. It was impossible to miss her delight. Now, he would help her dress and they would stop to complete his reason for visiting the coast before winging it home.

The moment he approached her belongings, Argenis was on alert. Men and women came out from the tree line bordering the beach. They held weapons in their hands as they dared to approach.

His roar of warning made them back up. Ciel sat up on his back and froze at the sight of the crowd.

"Hey, you! We're going to take your dragon," one angry-looking man called to Ciel.

*Pretend you are the one in charge. Meet their bluff with bravado.*

"Good luck with that. You know dragons will only attach themselves to virgins, right?" Ciel called. She knew Artemis could eliminate everyone with one massive burst of flame or simply launch into the air. She knew he was intrigued by their motivation.

The group looked at each other as if asking each other a silent question. She controlled her laugh when it seemed virgins were in short supply.

"Perhaps you could get him to do something for us?" one man requested.

"Trying to grab my dragon is a weird way of asking for a favor," Ciel pointed out. They might as well learn some manners.

One woman stepped out from the line into open space. "My apologies. I suggested that wasn't the wisest plan, but the men vetoed me. Thank you for not having your dragon roast us as a crunchy treat," she said, keeping her eyes on Ciel and Argenis but visibly rolling her eyes at her companions.

Ciel squashed the laughter that threatened. "What is the favor?"

"Our people are dying of thirst. We have the salty ocean water, but fresh water is far away. We need a trench to bring water closer. We will not survive digging it."

"Have you considered moving?" Ciel asked.

"It is too far. We will not survive the move either," the woman said, shaking her head.

Ciel looked at Argenis.

*This group chose not to offer mates to the dragons in their area eons ago. Both the dragons and the people have suffered from their ignorance.*

*I'm sure they aren't even aware their ancestors had a choice.*

Argenis nodded his agreement to that statement.

82

"He's going to help?" the woman said eagerly.

"No. He can help right a poor decision from the leaders of your past."

*Can you call to one of the dragons in this area?*

Argenis lifted his head and trumpeted a message into the sky.

Ciel watched everyone cower back except for the one woman who'd spoken. She stood bravely, waiting to see what happened. Ciel crossed her fingers, hoping for the best.

A massive red dragon appeared on the horizon. Its broad wings propelled it quickly through the sky. It circled over the beach as if curious before landing a distance from Argenis. In a familiar shimmering glow, it shifted into a very handsome silver-haired man.

"Why have you summoned me?"

Ciel watched the silent communication obviously taking place between the two dragon shifters. She was not privy to their conversation. Dragon business. She rolled her eyes.

The man looked toward the spokeswoman. "The assistance of dragons comes with a price."

"What kind of price?" the brave woman asked.

A young woman emerged from the greenery and walked forward as if drawn by an invisible thread. She walked past the woman standing on the sand.

"Chloe, no!" the spokeswoman said, trying to grab her arm.

"Mother. He calls to me." Chloe walked up to stand before the dragon shifter. His face had visibly softened, and he lifted one hand to cup her jaw. A wave of sexual tension and instant love burst from the two as he touched her, making Ciel's heart swell with happiness. There was no mistaking that this was his mate.

*Grab your clothes, Little Sky.*

Without questioning Argenis, Ciel followed his directions and scrambled onto his back.

"Wait! You are safe and happy?" the spokeswoman called to her, knowing that they would leave.

"Yes," Ciel called and held on as Argenis leapt into the sky.

She watched them over her shoulder for as long as she could. *We could have stayed.*

*An agreement will not be easy. Rough times are ahead.*

Ciel understood he was concerned for her safety. After a few seconds, she added, *I could feel their connection.*

*As could I. His was the most intact mind I found. There are other dragons in the area who have not fared as well without the balance a mate provides.*

*Like the black dragon?*

*Without a mate in the near future, Keres will become a threat to himself and others.*

*I think he'll find his mate soon*

*I hope you are correct, Little one.*

*Where to now, my magnificent mate? Home?*

*There is one stop I need to make.*

Knowing he'd chosen his words deliberately and wouldn't tell her more, Ciel chose to relax on Argenis's back rather than ask more questions. She shivered a bit in the cool air and wished she'd had time to change from her bikini. Instantly, the scales below her heated to warm her.

*Perfect!* She wadded up the clothes and tucked them under her body to keep them safe.

She watched as they approached a large city. The massive skyscrapers reached into the clouds. *How are they surviving?* The streets were clogged with nonfunctional buses, taxis, and cars. The smell was not pleasant even from above. Ciel pinched her nose.

People milled around on the street below. She couldn't tell if they were actually doing something or just wandering. Suddenly, Ciel was very thankful for being part of a small community that had rallied together.

To her relief, Argenis flew over the city without stopping. When the path below turned into an industrial area, he descended. The large parking area was mostly deserted, with all the junk vehicles pushed to the far side.

*What could you want here?*

Seconds after the question left her mind, Ciel saw a man walk out with a cloth wrapped around his mouth.

"Don't bring your Little here. There's an illness here. I think it's the water," the man called.

Instantly bristling at the thought that Argenis had shared her secret, Ciel glared at the beast in front of her.

*Calm yourself, Little one. He addresses you like this because I'm here on business. Climb down, please.*

Descending, she sent him a *harrumph!*

*I am noting your unhappiness and disrespectfulness.*

*Wait? Am I in trouble?*

Argenis didn't answer, but shifted to his human form. "Stay here, Ciel."

She crossed her fingers as he approached the man in front of them. Could dragons get sick?

Straining her ears, she tried to hear what they were discussing. She could tell from the man's posture that he was unwell. Her heart ached at the thought of everyone suffering from all the challenges and illnesses cropping up in the aftermath of the big change.

Argenis turned and scanned the parking lot. She suspected he was looking for any threat. His gaze met hers.

*Scream or make noise.*

She nodded.

Argenis walked forward and disappeared inside the building.

The breeze over her skin reminded her she still wore her bikini. Quickly, she put on her shorts and T-shirt. Ciel stuffed the bra and panties into her pocket. The swimsuit would replace them for a while.

Ciel watched the door, waiting for him to return. It was just a few minutes but felt like forever. When he appeared, Argenis carried a large package balanced on his shoulder. She knew that was the reason for their trip away from Wyvern.

Ater trying to figure out what could be in the brown cardboard box and giving up, Ciel noticed the other man had not reappeared. She hoped that wasn't a bad sign. When Argenis was about halfway to her, he exploded into flames.

"Argenis!"

She rushed forward several steps before noting that the fiery figure kept moving forward. Bad movies flashed into her brain, and she took several steps backward. Ciel prepared to turn and run. She froze in place as the fire died out.

Argenis emerged unscathed and nude. Mesmerized by his powerful body striding across the parking lot on full display, she tried not to look at his private parts while staring at the same time.

*Oh, what big eyes you have, Little Sky!*

Ciel could feel her face heating and knew that she was blushing. Forcing herself to raise her focus above his body, she noticed burned wispy bits of paper floating to the ground. They appeared to be the destroyed packaging around the box on his shoulder. The part that remained was sooty, with bits gleaming in the sunlight.

"What is that?" she asked.

"Something for your birthday."

"My birthday? I don't even know what day it is."

When he set it on the pavement and continued forward, she asked, "Can I see it?"

"Not yet."

In a flash, he resumed his dragon form. When he lowered his head, she knew she was supposed to climb up on his shoulders. The allure of the object before them made her try to dart around him to see what it was.

"Eek!"

Argenis caught the back of her shorts easily in his mouth and lifted her off the pavement. Bending his long neck, he placed her on his back. *In position, Little one.*

She felt him move forward and watched him grab that mysterious item with his claws. Feeling his muscles bunch, she scurried into position. In a flash, he was back in the clouds.

# Chapter 13

Waiting for her birthday was interminable. She had two more days to find out what Argenis had collected for her.

Trying to entertain herself, she enjoyed playing her new favorite game—guess what's in that sooty container.

She knew Argenis had used his fire inside to harden a large vat, making it possible for the community to boil water to make it safe. The grateful man had given him the package. Ciel had some hint that her gift hadn't been there by accident. Argenis had gone to get it and then helped.

By combusting his body and the gift after leaving the area of illness, Argenis eliminated all the germs he might have encountered. And given her a show that she had replayed in her memory many times already. Watching him stride toward her—all hard muscles and manliness. Mmmm!

She'd decided to look around. If she happened to find the container, it wouldn't be her fault he was a bad hider.

Wandering through his immense home, Ciel couldn't believe that she still got lost as she explored. How crazy was that? Thank goodness there was a central hallway that ran from the front to the back.

Today, she chose to start in the library. Argenis often worked in the gorgeous room. Since he was out surveying the land around Wyvern, she had free rein to check it out without worrying about bothering him. A huge tome that appeared to be the twin of the one passed down to her lay open on an elegant walnut and metal bookstand. She ran her fingers down the hand-inked designs. They certainly didn't create books like that anymore.

Walking along the bookcases that lined the room, she spotted famous authors and works she'd only heard of but never read. Many who had been gone for years. There was not a speck of dust on the shelves, and each book was in pristine condition. Selecting one, she peeked at the inside cover just to see if anyone had ever opened it. She froze seeing the signature of the author and her mate's name. Carefully, she set that back into place, knowing the value of that one volume had to be significant.

On the last bookshelf, there was a beautifully carved heart ornament. Ciel picked it up and panicked when she heard the faint grinding of gears. Crap! What had she done? Quickly, she replaced the wooden heart, and the noise stopped.

Staring at that decoration, she battled with herself, trying to squash the temptation to touch it again. Ciel looked over her shoulder and listened intently for anyone in the area. The house was quiet.

Cautiously, she reached for the wooden object again. This time, she pulled it against her chest and held it. Again, that distinctive sound happened. Where was it coming from? She pressed her ear to the wooden frame of the bookcase and listened.

*Yes!* It was coming from there.

She stepped back to scan the books displayed in front of

her and gasped. One section was partially ajar, pushed out into the room. Ciel raised the box to set it back on the shelf and saw the opening narrow. It was linked somehow to the object in her hand.

Ciel stepped to the couch and set the box on the end table next to a gorgeous Tiffany lamp as she eyed the door. It reopened. Obviously, this wasn't a passage meant for random people to explore. She wasn't just anyone, though, right?

Gathering her courage, Ciel walked to the opening and pulled it to create a large enough space she could squeeze through. Without allowing herself to chicken out, she stepped into the hidden passage and immediately let out a short shriek as she batted the cobwebs from her hair. Obviously, the housekeepers didn't come this way.

She squared her shoulders and forged on, batting the wispy threads out of her way as she walked down a metal spiral staircase. It was musty and dim. The perfect setting for a horror movie. *Now why did I think of that?* Ciel tried to shake that thought out of her mind with very limited success.

Spooked, she forced herself to keep going. Argenis would never have anything dangerous in his house. She'd be fine.

A scream burst from her lips when she turned a corner and came face to face with a bear—its mouth gaping open with white teeth trying to bite her. Ciel ran up several steps before realizing she didn't hear anything behind her. Panting, she paused and held her breath to listen. Nothing.

Quietly, she snuck down the steps. The bear hadn't moved. She waved a hand to see if he could see her. There was no reaction from the creature. Ciel poked at the bear and felt real fur. Stuffed. Who put a huge attacking bear in the stairwell of his secret passage?

Argenis, of course.

"I hope he ate you," she scolded the bear and jumped

when her voice echoed. Prepared for anything now, she carefully snuck past the bear. It was dead, but she wasn't taking any chances.

Her next find was a faded photo of a beautiful woman. She held a locket around her neck that was shaped like a heart. Suspecting this was one of Argenis's former mates, Ciel wanted to hate her, but the woman looked so happy. Ciel couldn't keep from feeling glad that Argenis had enjoyed this woman's company and love.

Feeling less scared and more intrigued, she continued. The stairs ended in a vast room. Ciel figured this must be the basement under the mansion. Here and there were scattered boxes and old pieces of furniture draped by dust cloths.

There was one couch without fabric covering it. Ciel walked toward it and discovered displayed in front of the seating area were beautifully ornate picture frames with a combination of portraits and photos. The woman from the stairs appeared again alongside two other women and one handsome man.

Moving closer to the latter, Ciel was eager to see what Argenis had looked like years ago. She inhaled sharply at the sight of deep red hair, a mustache, and dark brown eyes that seemed to see into her soul. That was not Argenis. Scanning the portrait of the well-muscled man, Ciel noted something special.

Her gaze darted from one framed picture to the next. Every person wore the same type of necklace. Each different. But all consisted of a heart-shaped locket.

"You have been busy, mate."

Ciel whirled to see Argenis standing behind her. "I'm sorry. I should have asked before coming down here."

He nodded to agree with her but remained silent, giving her courage. Maybe she wasn't in trouble.

"Who are they?" she asked.

"This is my place to remember my mates. I come here every once in a while to think of them and treasure the time we had together. Not because I'm unhappy with my life in the present, but because they were so important to me, I don't want to forget their impact on my life."

"One's a man..."

"Love doesn't know a gender, Ciel. Neither does a mate bond. I don't know who was more surprised, Edward or myself. Does it bother you that one of my mates was male?" Argenis asked, studying her face.

Ciel shook her head. "No. It's... It's actually quite hot."

Argenis laughed and nodded.

"Was it a huge scandal?"

"More than being mated to a dragon alone? I don't believe so. As you can tell, Edward was as strong as a mule. He was sometimes as stubborn as one. The town's citizens didn't argue with him."

"Tell me about her. I saw her on the stairs," Ciel requested, pointing to one of the pictures..

"Come sit with me, Little Sky. I'll tell you about everyone if you are interested," he invited as he sat on the couch. When Ciel approached eagerly, he lifted her onto his lap, turning her so she could see his face as well as the portraits.

"Her name is Marianne. She was my third mate, the daughter of the town's storekeeper. She was quick-witted and eager to experience life."

"That portrait is of Helena, my first mate. As soon as the pact was signed in blood, we bonded. I handed the quill back to her, and the mark appeared when our hands touched. She was forty. Unwed. The town's healer who had urged the town's folk to consider the pact."

"Forty was old then, wasn't it?"

"Ancient," he agreed. "Her mind was an amazing store-house of facts about nature and healing. Her book sits on my shelf."

"Is that Everly?"

"Yes. She's been gone for almost twenty years now."

"Do you miss her?" Ciel had to ask.

"I miss all of them, but I am not so foolish as to lose my focus on the one I am lucky enough to have in my life now. They were all special. You are the mate I lavish my love on now."

"Do you love me?" she asked.

"With all my heart." Argenis pulled her toward him and kissed her lips softly, before adding, "I have a present for you in the library. I was waiting for your birthday, but I think this would be a good time for you to have it. Do you have any more questions for me before we leave this spot?"

"No. Thank you for telling me about them."

"Of course."

"Will you put me on your wall?" she asked.

"I have found an artist to paint your picture. He will be here next week."

"That's fun," she said, instantly intrigued by the idea.

"I have a feeling you will find it very tedious to sit still for hours," he commented with a smile.

"Hours? That doesn't sound fun," she said, changing her mind.

"It will be worth it when it's finished. How many people do you know who have their portraits painted?" he pointed out.

"Zero."

"It's always a good idea to remember sitting on a hot bottom would be even more difficult."

"You'd spank me if I fidget?" she asked, aghast.

"Oh, yes."

Studying his face, she knew he was telling the truth. "Did you spank them?" she asked, waving a hand toward the wall.

"Yes."

"Even Edward?"

"Frequently. He frequently put himself in danger's way."

Ciel looked at him and nodded. "I could see that happen —the danger, not the spanking."

Argenis boosted Ciel to her feet and took her hand. She pulled back when he led her away from the stairs. "Isn't it this way?" she asked.

"Only if you want to battle the spiders."

She ran a hand over her hair at the thought of having picked up a creepy crawler from the webs. "There's a different way?"

"Yes, Little Sky. Come with me. This mansion is old and holds many secrets," he told her as they walked away from the spiral staircase. "It also has been updated."

She stared at an elevator standing with its doors open. "Does that work?"

"By dragon power, yes."

He ushered her inside and placed her in the far corner. One section of the elevator's wall was missing. Ciel could see the cables running up and down. As she watched, Argenis heaved on one and they rose three feet. Again and again, he tugged on the lines. When they came to the next floor, he tied off the cables and pushed open the door.

"I couldn't do that myself," she said, mind boggled by his strength.

"This is very definitely a 'do not try this at home' moment. Come on, your gift is in my desk."

She looked at what had seemed to be a supply closet in the hall and shook her head before allowing him to lead her back to his office. Standing by his desk, Ciel watched him sit in the big leather chair to pull something out from under his desk.

It was the charred box she'd seen before when he'd torched all his clothing away. She hadn't focused much on it with all that delicious scenery. Ciel wrinkled her nose at the sight of the tarnished box.

Argenis opened the latch and drew the top back on a hinge. Inside, it was gorgeous. Ciel leaned forward to peer closer. Lined in purple plush, it looked like the most extravagant jewelry box ever. She saw one gleaming item inside.

"Here it is." He lifted a delicate necklace off the velvet. "I started this tradition several hundred years ago. I would love for you to wear this, my mate." He stood before holding it out for her to see.

Ciel traced the delicate chain. Intrigued, she looked closer. "Are the links dragons?"

"Silver dragons."

"That is gorgeous, Daddy."

"Would you like to wear it, Little Sky? Once it is on, you will never take it off," he warned.

"Never? What if I'm going swimming or wearing a gold dress?"

"The metal is waterproof. And you will never wear a gold dress." The last was in a tone that brooked no argument.

"I like gold. I have a bunch of gold earrings and a killer pair of stilettos," she told him.

"We will find another home for your treasures."

"What?"

"Back to the necklace," he suggested.

"Oh, I'm sorry. It's beautiful. Does the locket mean something?" She thought she should double check.

"That you are the beloved mate of the silver dragon and under my protection."

Her eyes filled with tears as her emotions overwhelmed her. "That's so sweet. And I was worried about clashing with my clothes."

"Would you like to wear this, Ciel?" he repeated patiently.

"Yes," she answered, smiling.

He placed the beautiful jewelry around her neck and fiddled with the front before smoothing it on her collarbones. "Perfect."

"They all had them," she said, running her fingers over the cool metal that warmed quickly against her skin.

"Yes."

Argenis pulled her close and pressed his lips against hers in a gentle kiss that quickly ignited. She squirmed closer to him, enjoying the feel of his body against hers. He cupped her bottom and aligned her pelvis with his, skyrocketing her arousal.

"How do I respond so strongly to you?" she wondered.

"You are my mate. My body calls to you and yours to mine." He rubbed her soft mound against his rapidly hardening shaft.

She linked her arms around his neck and asked, "Make love to me, mate?"

"What do you think I'm doing?" he asked with a grin before tracing a finger down the side of her neck to the locket. She shivered and wiggled away.

"Are you okay, Little one?"

"I keep thinking about those spider webs. Do you think I have any spiders on me?"

"We should definitely check."

His hands lifted her T-shirt over her head. Ciel clasped her hands over her breasts as she looked at the open door.

"Do not hide from me, Ciel," Argenis reprimanded her sternly as he unfastened her jean shorts.

"Argenis! Anyone could walk by."

"Daddy."

"Okay, Daddy, anyone could walk by," she said, exasperated. She wiggled her hips, trying to stop him as he pulled down her shorts and panties.

"My staff is well trained. They will not intrude. There is a spider here. On your sock."

"What? Get it off!" she begged. Her hands dropped from her breast to whisk over her arms. If there was one, there were more.

"It's only a little one, Ciel. I'll take care of this."

In a short time, she stood nude in front of him. He looked over her body carefully before having her turn to show him her back.

Looking over her shoulder, she asked, "Do you see any more?"

"Not yet, Ciel. I need to check one more place. Arms behind your back. Now, lean over my desk," he requested.

Willing to do anything to make sure she didn't have spiders on her, Ciel moved to loom over the papers on his desk. She gasped in surprise when he lifted her to adjust her position. Reaching down with her toes, she discovered she could barely graze her big toe on the carpet. She tried to scoot back, but he wrapped one hand around her hands still clasped behind her back. He held her securely in place as he sat down in his chair.

"Spread your legs."

"I don't have any spiders there," she protested.

"I haven't checked."

She quickly moved her thighs apart. He inserted his knees between hers and pushed them further apart.

"Beautiful." He stroked his hand over the curve of her bottom. He rubbed his thumb on that sensitive spot where her bottom met her thighs. "Good news. No more spiders. Yet."

"I don't even want to think about that," she said, hearing a drawer open.

"I'll need both hands, Little Sky."

She felt something cold hook around her wrists, securing her overlapped hands together in that same location behind her back. Immediately, she tried to pull her arms loose since he wasn't holding her. "Let me go, Argenis."

"Daddy. I haven't finished my search. I think you need a reminder to call me Daddy, Little one."

Looking over her shoulder, she watched him pull a tube of lubricant out of his desk and a small object that made her meet his gaze in shock. "You can't put that in my bottom."

"Of course I can. You need stretching anyway so you don't tear. A plug in your bottom will remind you to call me Daddy. After you wear it a few times, you'll remember," he explained as he spread her cheeks to look at the small entrance between them.

She tried to turn over, but he easily held her in place. "I have bigger plugs if you're naughty."

Ciel flattened herself against the desk.

"Good girl."

Argenis twisted off the seal of the lubricant and opened the jar. When she saw his finger emerge from the jar with a big dollop of a thick substance, Ciel pressed her forehead against the cool wood. She bit her lip as he dabbed the cool mixture on her tight ring of muscles before pressing that digit deep inside her.

She didn't know what to do. It felt awful, amazing, hot, and embarrassing all at the same time. Closing her eyes, she tried to think of something else. A moan fell from her mouth as he applied the slippery mixture inside. Each movement seemed to fire up a million nerve endings. *Please don't let him notice I'm wet.*

"Eventually, Daddy will put his cock in your bottom, Little Sky. Are you brave enough to take me?"

"Not today!" she wailed.

"Okay. Soon," he promised, and she knew she'd just agreed.

She needed to stop talking. It was hard to think with his finger inside her bottom. When he finally drew it slowly out, she flattened to the desk. A few seconds later, the feel of something cold against that puckered entrance made her inhale sharply and contract her bottom with all her forces.

"None of that, Little Sky. Relax your bottom. A plug is going into your bottom. The longer you delay, the more likely someone will come to find me."

She looked desperately at the door. Still open. "Could you close the door, Daddy?"

"Relax and I will close the door on my way out to wash my hands."

Nodding quickly, Ciel tried to relax.

"Take a deep breath and blow it out slowly. One, two, three, four, five. That's a very good girl," he praised her as he seated the plug against that small ring of muscles. He patted her bottom as he slid a drawer out of his desk. "You stay right there, and I'll be back."

She watched him close the door as he left. As time ticked by, the thought of getting up popped into her mind. Ciel tugged her hands. There was no way she could unfasten those or get dressed without her hands. She tried to pull her thighs together to be less on display and discovered there was something keeping her from doing that. He'd pulled the center drawer out.

*He knows me too well.*

Hearing the murmur of voices out in the hall, Ciel could tell someone had caught Argenis before he could return. "I'll need an hour first and then I can definitely take over at the east barricade." There was a mumble for a response, and then she heard the door reopen.

"There's my beautiful girl," he said as he returned to her side. Once retaking his seat, he pushed the drawer back inside.

"That was mean."

"Oh? You tried to move?" he asked with a deceptive lightness that she knew better than to fall for.

"No. It scratched the inside of my thigh."

"Oh, no. I'll treat that so it doesn't become infected," he assured her as he stood.

Before she could let out an eep, he had turned her over to lie on her back. Her arms ached instantly underneath her, but that was not distressing as the device in her bottom. Instinctively, she tried to pull her legs together as the plug shifted to remind her it was there. His hands pressed her knees back into position. "Sorry."

"You are forgiven. Now, let's look at this scratch."

He searched diligently over her inner thighs. His fingers skating dangerously close to the area, she suddenly wanted him to touch more than anything. "I'm not finding anything."

"Maybe it just felt like a scratch."

"Perhaps." His fingers brushed through her trimmed pubic hair. When her hips bucked upward, he pressed her pelvis back down.

Ciel moaned as the exterior flange of the plug hit the wooden desk.

"You do need Daddy's attention. Let me kiss it and make it better."

Expecting him to kiss the alleged scratch on her inner thigh, she moaned as his mouth pressed a kiss to her pussy. She closed her eyes at the feel of his tongue tasting her arousal juices. His hum of approval sent vibrations through her.

Without lifting his mouth from her pussy, Argenis lifted one of her legs to set her foot on the edge of the desk before repeating his action for the other. With her splayed out before him, her mate settled himself between her thighs to nibble and taste. He seemed to know just where she needed him to touch and played her body like a finely-tuned instrument. When he pulled her clit into his mouth as he sucked lightly on it, Argenis pressed two fingers into her.

A keening scream filled the room. It took a fraction of a second for Ciel to process that she was the source of the sound. Embarrassed, she bit her lip to cut off the noise.

"Daddy wants to hear all your noises, Little Sky," he reprimanded her.

"I don't do anything right," she accused, overwhelmed by all the sensations buffeting her.

"That is not true. Just the sight of you tempts me, Ciel." He pulled his fingers from her pussy and licked them clean.

"I could taste you on my fingers every day for the next one hundred years and want more. Soon you'll realize that I will demand everything from you." He tapped the outer guard of the plug to jostle it in her bottom. "As I take you in every way possible to bring us both pleasure."

Her body gushed at that thought. She met his eyes as he stood once again between her legs. He walked around the desk and pulled her body across the surface of the wood until her head dangled fully over the edge. She could only focus on his hands as he unfastened his belt and pushed his trousers and boxers down his legs. His massive cock was directly in her line of vision.

She watched him drag his hand from root to tip. Licking her lips without thinking, Ciel did it again when she heard him groan. He stepped forward to rub the velvety soft head across her lips. Wishing a taste, she darted her tongue out to taste him.

"Good girl. Open your mouth."

Immediately, she parted her lips, inviting him inside. He pressed slowly into the heat of her mouth, challenging her ability to take him completely without hesitation. He believed in her. She did her best and felt him glide out just as she knew she couldn't take any more.

"Your mouth feels amazing around my cock. A little deeper this time. Swallow," he coached her as he pushed into her throat and then groaned as she followed his instructions.

"So good. That deserves a reward, right? I think it should start right about now."

As if on cue, a buzzing started, and the vibrations reverberated through her body. He thrust more forcefully into her mouth as she tried to figure out what was happening. A wet slapping sound registered first before the zing of sensations flooded her pussy. The plug.

"It's hard to concentrate on everything, isn't it, Little one?"

*"How—How does it even work?"* she thought to herself, unable to ask him.

"It's old-fashioned tech, Little Sky. Wind up technology that doesn't need any batteries. The timer has a delay. There's a surprise before it stops working."

She couldn't nod as he filled her mouth once again. His hands seemed to be everywhere on her body. A tweak to her nipple almost pushed her into a second orgasm, but she was determined to wait for his.

This time, when he almost withdrew completely before flexing his hips to drive himself into her mouth, she could taste the flavor of his cum and knew that he was close. Sealing her lips around him, she sucked him deep and tried to make it difficult for him to glide out.

The buzzing inside her increased, and Ciel clenched her fingers together, trying to hold on as she feasted on his thick shaft. His shout into the room gave her permission to come, and she felt everything inside her shatter as he thrust into her mouth and emptied himself down her throat.

Long minutes later, she sat on his lap with an empty bottom and a blown mind as he rocked her slowly. "Can you even fly after that? I don't think I know my own name."

"I'll manage. Do you know my name now?"

"Daddy," she said contentedly.

"There's my good girl. Would you like to nap in your nursery with Silly while I go on patrol?"

"Yes, please." Her eyes simply wouldn't stay open.

Holding her shielded against his chest, Argenis strolled naked through the house. No one looked at them or even seemed to notice as they walked by. He tucked her in her bed and pressed a kiss to her mouth before pressing another to the heart locket around her throat.

"Such a good girl. Daddy loves you."

"Night, Daddy."

She didn't hear him walk out of the nursery.

# Chapter 14

"Happy birthday, Little Sky."

Blinking her eyes open, Ciel looked into her Daddy's crystal-clear, light blue eyes. "Hi, Daddy."

"Are you ready to get up and enjoy your day?"

"Or you could get in bed with me, and we could snuggle with Silly?" she suggested.

"That does sound appealing, but perhaps I could tempt you. The cook has made your favorite breakfast."

"Waffles with strawberries and whipped cream?"

"Waffles with fresh peaches and whipped cream, courtesy of a woman with a sore whipping arm. I know I hate it when that happens," he joked, delivering a slap on her bottom.

"Daddy!"

"Isn't there a human tradition where the birthday girl gets a spank for every year they've been alive?"

"Let's not worry about weird human traditions. I'm with you now. Everything is totally different. Besides, waffles with peaches are so close to those with strawberries in my list of favorites. It's a perfect silver dragon's mate tradition."

He scooped her out of bed and stood to twirl her around. Ciel could keep from laughing at his antics. "Stop, Daddy. You're going to make me dizzy," she pleaded as the world whirled around.

Instantly, he froze, holding her close. "I'll charge one kiss."

Ciel nodded and leaned forward to press her lips to his. Allowing her control of the kiss, Argenis responded to her every action. When she brushed her tongue across his lower lip, he opened his mouth to grant her access. She hummed with pleasure at his flavor.

When he lifted his head, she licked her lips very deliberately, drawing a groan from deep within him.

"You are a temptress, Little Sky." He squeezed her bottom as he held her before adding, "No delaying! Think of the whipped cream on top of the fruit."

"We can't let that go to waste. Maybe there would be some fluffy stuff left over. I might not have tried my favorite thing to eat," she suggested with a flirtatious tilt of her head as she trailed one finger down the center of his torso.

That earned her a full, two-second stare as he appeared to consider her suggestion. When her smile became a grin, he shook his head and tossed Ciel up on his shoulder.

"Potty!" she alerted him as her weight settled on her bladder.

Without asking a single question, he took long strides to hurry to the bathroom as he slid her back down into his arms. Argenis set her feet on the tile and let her run to the toilet. Collapsing on the seat, she relaxed her muscles.

It had seemed so weird to have him in the bathroom with her while she peed in the beginning. There were no boundaries with Argenis. She was his.

When she finished, Ciel joined him at the sink where he

waited. She stood naked, facing the mirror as he brushed the tangles from her hair.

"Ponytail or braid?"

"Braid," she answered definitively.

"One or two?"

"Two into one?" she asked to challenge him.

He simply nodded and divided her hair into two sections at the top. Argenis didn't seem concerned about the difficulty level of that request. "Purple ribbon?"

"Yes, please. Daddy, what's your favorite hairstyle to do?"

"Mohawk. You know I'm great with a razor."

"A mohawk? I can't do that." She looked at him in shock, knowing her jaw had dropped at that mental image.

"Then I guess we do my almost number one."

"The two braids into one suggestion?" she asked, suspecting he was teasing her.

"Exactly."

He braided her hair quickly and smoothly. She loved that Argenis never tugged her scalp.

Standing there naked was awkward. Facing the mirror while he finished, she couldn't avoid looking at her body reflected in the mirror. The longer she looked at herself, the more anxious she became. She was not a raving beauty. What could he see in her?

She forced her gaze to focus on other things in his bathroom. Sure, that even a bathroom could tell you a lot about the person who decorated it, Ciel looked around. There was a professional flower arrangement in the niche on the far wall. A decorator must have chosen those.

"Tell me what you're thinking about, Little Sky," he asked softly.

"I don't think you selected that vase thing," Ciel rushed to say, pointing over her shoulder and getting turned around by the mirror's reflection. In the process, she flailed around a lot, demonstrating all her flaws like untoned arms and breasts that sure didn't look like the perky stacked ones famous, beautiful people had.

"I didn't choose that. That space was created in the last makeover. I told the designer I didn't want one, but she was sure I'd change my mind. I think Abby, my housekeeper, picked that up for a couple of bucks at a garage sale in Wyvern."

Argenis paused to wrap a scrunchie around the bottom of the braid before admitting, "I didn't notice it for a couple of weeks. The staff had a pot going on and took bets on how long it would take me to comment on it."

"Who won?"

"The head gardener. All right. I'm all done."

"Thank goodness. Remind me to put on some clothes before I stand here staring at all my..." She stopped talking as his expression changed from amusement to concern to displeasure.

"Sorry. I didn't mean to point out my flaws."

That didn't make his expression lighten. "Little Sky. Your body is strong and healthy. It is also beautiful and desirable. I entertained myself while fixing your hair by listing all the things I could bend you over to fuck you."

"What?" she whispered, sure he must be making that up.

"Twenty-seven places on the first floor. Want to know about the second?"

She shook her head in disbelief. "Come on, Argenis. Your other mates were drop-dead gorgeous."

"And you are not?" he asked with a dark glower.

"Of course not. I'm average. The only thing remarkable about me is my hair. It's nice."

"Whoa, Little one. You are looking at yourself through a

whole different filter than I am. I think you need a lesson before waffles."

"Maybe I should skip the waffles," she said with a laugh, poking a finger at her slightly rounded stomach.

"Close your eyes, Ciel. Let's go check out that door between our minds."

"Have I been thinking too much at you?" she asked, afraid that she'd bothered him.

"No, Little Sky. The touch of your mind is always the favorite part of my day. Second to hugging you in person. Now, close your eyes. Look for the silver flash. Can you see it?"

She'd followed his directions haphazardly. It would at least look like she was following his directions. That was always a much better idea than getting in trouble. Ciel searched but couldn't find the silver. "Sorry," she answered after a short time and opened her eyes.

His immense hand covered the top half of her face, forcing her to shut her lids completely. "Look now."

Shrugging inwardly, she wondered how he always knew everything. A zing of silver jolted through her line of vision. Quickly, she chased it. "There!"

"Good girl. Follow it. Don't get distracted. There's a difference between silver and white."

"I know that. This one is silver."

"I'm going to link my mind with yours," he warned and a split second later, she felt the arousing touch of Argenis's mind. He always felt so amazingly right it turned her on instantly. "Silver, Little Sky. Don't let me distract you."

"Oops."

She searched around for the silver light. "There." Concentrating with everything she had, Ciel followed its trail to that impressive door she'd visited before.

"Open the third lock."

From his voice alone, she could tell this was important. Hesitantly, she reached out to turn the last one. With a pop, the door burst open. Struck by a million sensations, Ciel stiffened against Argenis. This was overwhelming.

"Take a deep breath, Little one. You're fine. Think about something silly to ground you. How does my little finger feel?"

She gathered everything together and forced her way through to find his body, then his arm, hand, wrist, fingers, pinky. Ciel laughed.

"It's always wanted to stick out in the proper English fashion at a tea party," she reported.

"Let's try something a bit harder. Don't open your eyes, but focus on mine."

She retraced her steps and headed to his handsome face. Tripping over the muscles bunched here and there, Ciel couldn't believe how strong he felt. There was more than just power. Overlaid in every sinew of muscle was the dragon. She forced herself to his eyes and froze.

Argenis didn't have his eyes closed. He looked straight into the mirror at her nude form. She felt a gush of arousal flood her pussy. She'd never imagined she could look so good—delicious. Her best qualities combined to create a sensuous creature she found extremely desirable.

As she watched, he lifted a hand from the vanity and stroked over her ribcage. She inhaled sharply as his thumb brushed over her skin. It felt like warm velvet under his touch. He skimmed past the side swell of her breasts. Her mouth watered from his memories of how her breasts felt when he nuzzled and sucked on them. And she'd thought it was phenomenal from her perspective.

She could eavesdrop on his mind as Argenis considered

all the ways he could explore her body and what he wanted to do to her. Her dragon shifter had a very creative mind. Some of his thoughts shocked her. All of them turned her on.

He refocused on her face and scanned down her body, showing her he couldn't see any of the flaws she imagined. She couldn't believe how lovely she looked. She'd never felt so beautiful and desirable.

His hand moved again, cherishing the gentle curve of her stomach that was so erotic to feel against the chiseled six-pack he sported. Sliding through the slick arousal that coated her intimate spaces, his feeling of arousal multiplied the sensations she felt as he skillfully caressed her.

Argenis supported her as he moved her legs apart with nudges. Her weight was so minuscule, he didn't even consider it. All those times, he'd carried her ricocheted into her mind and she felt his reaction—caring, nurturing, tender. Totally Daddy.

"My precious, cherished mate. Do you wish to close the door and go have waffles or..." He paused for just a second as his fingers played between her thighs. "Or should we make love first and have lunch later?"

Ciel astounded herself as she leaned forward to place her forearms on the vanity and wiggle her bottom at him. "I'm totally hungry for something not waffle related."

The pleasure on his face at her daring words quickly disappeared as he stepped forward to glide his cock through the slick juices of her pussy as his hands caressed her hips. Feeling his sensations as well as hers was incredible. Her pink folds felt like warm, wet velvet across his cock. The ache in his shaft and balls revealed his desire and urgent need to fill her.

"In me, please," she begged, meeting his eyes in the

mirror and loving the silver flash that signaled how close his dragon was to the surface.

He wrapped his fingers around the base of his cock and placed himself at her entrance. The anticipation in each of them made the second delay seem like a lifetime. When he thrust forward, filling her with a single motion, Ciel almost blacked out from the avalanche of emotions and feelings. Argenis supported her as he loomed over her body, holding her gaze with his.

If two minds could meld together, that's what Ciel would swear happened. Tender and demanding, Argenis demanded all that she could give and took everything. She could only feel and react. Each touch and sensation etched itself into her brain as he made love to her.

When their heartbeats settled a long time later, Ciel could barely keep her eyes open. She struggled to close that door again, even with his coaching. It was not feasible to keep it open. The pleasure would be too addictive. When it was resealed, she could focus on other things besides how much she loved Argenis.

Ciel clung to his shoulders as he carried her back to the bed. Following her under the covers, he made her first birthday wish come true as they lazed together with Silly.

"Best birthday ever," she whispered before falling back to sleep against his chest.

# Chapter 15

Her stomach growling woke them both up. Laughing, Argenis threw her back over his shoulder and toted her to the bathroom as they replayed how their day had started initially. This time, however, he steered her into the shower after she pottied to freshen up.

With a quick smoothing hand to her braids, Argenis led her into the closet.

"Clothes and then food. Pink, blue, or purple today?"

"Purple," she answered without hesitating.

"Daddy's choice or Ciel's choice?"

"Daddy's." It was always so much easier if she let him select something. He had the best taste anyway.

In a few minutes, she wore a pair of flowered leggings in a beautiful pattern with a solid T-shirt of the exact same color of dark purple. She watched him cover up his chiseled body with trousers and a silky crewneck shirt, both enjoying the look of him in fashionable clothing and missing the view.

*Thank goodness he can't still hear all my thoughts.*

His slow wink as he placed a hand on her lower back to guide her to the kitchen made her wonder. He couldn't, could he? Her stomach grumbled again, making them both laugh as she pressed a hand to her abdomen.

"Come on, Little Sky. If we wait much longer, you're going to be ready for a roasted rack of dragon."

"Never!" she promised, appalled by that thought.

"I'll hold you to that."

Entering the kitchen, they discovered waffles were still available if they wanted them. The cook suggested a southern delight of fried chicken and waffles.

"I've heard of that but never tried it," she said with a smile.

In a few minutes, they had freshly crafted waffles piled with battered chicken strips. Served with hot maple syrup and butter, the combination tasted better than Ciel had expected. She ate more than she'd ever thought possible.

"I can't put another bite in my mouth," she confessed, tossing her napkin on to the table as she leaned back in her chair with a groan.

Seeing Argenis's empty plate, she lifted hers and offered it to him. "Can you finish this? I hate to see that deliciousness going to waste."

It was gone in a flash.

"So what would you like to do for your birthday, Little Sky?" he asked.

"Could I see my present?"

"You think I got you a present?" he teased.

"Daddy!"

"You've waited long enough, I suppose. Come with me."

Standing, Argenis held out his hand for hers and led her to the library. Ciel felt her cheeks blush at the sight of the desk with papers pushed off onto the floor. He dealt with those quickly before leaning under the desk to pull out a gift wrapped in shiny silver wrapping paper.

"That was there yesterday?"

"It was. We never got under the desk. Perhaps next time," he suggested with a knowing smile.

She didn't know what to say to that, so she focused on the gift. "Can I open it now?"

"Please do." He set it on his desk, and she rushed to the other side to tear open the package.

"Oh!" The air caught in her throat as she revealed an ornate silver box. The size of four shoe boxes stacked together, the silver gleamed with an almost blinding gleam. A finely detailed dragon wrapped around the box as decoration with his head and gleaming ice-blue eyes on top to guard the treasure inside. She was almost afraid to touch it in fear of damaging it.

"It's beautiful. But it's too much. I can't accept this."

"You can. Do you not want it?"

"It's gorgeous. I don't know what it is?" she admitted.

"Open it." When she hesitated a few centimeters from touching it, he assured her, "You will not hurt it. It's hardier than you think."

Cautiously, she lifted the lid, finding that it tilted back. The inside was lined with the lightest blue velvet. Unable to resist, she ran her finger over the soft fabric. "Nice. It's a jewelry box?" she asked, seeing the divisions for rings and other fancy adornments.

"It is. I think it shined up very nicely, don't you? It took a couple hours of dragon sweat and tears to take the tarnish off. The finest silversmith in the colonies made that jewelry box."

"Like the US colonies?" she questioned, unable to believe it could be that old. She carefully pulled her fingers from the box.

"Yes."

While she digested that, he added, "Empty jewelry boxes are incredibly sad. Let's go find something to make it happy."

He lifted the box from the desk and placed it on his shoulder. As Argenis reached for her hand, a memory flashed into her mind at the similar sight.

"That was what you got after we went swimming!"

"You are correct. The jewelry box was a new find for me. I took it to an expert to have it relined and then everything happened. As it was, I rescued it before they could melt it down for the precious metal."

"Do you think they are doing better?" she asked.

"I know so. I had Keres scare the hell out of them."

"That made them feel better?" she asked, studying his face.

"No. The water sterilization supplies he delivered to them did that." Argenis tugged her hand gently to get her to walk with him.

"You're a nice guy," she said as they left the library and went down the hall. He stopped at that massive metal door with all the locks. "Let's check in here to see if there is anything for your jewelry box."

"I already have my locket," she reminded him.

"Yes. But that doesn't come off your neck, Little Sky. We need other things for your jewelry collection."

She watched him open the lock with keys from a huge keyring he produced from somewhere. When he pushed open the door, she peeked into the area behind it and walked inside, mesmerized.

"I don't even know what to say," she whispered.

Ciel couldn't even see the far end of the room. Here and there were collections of precious items. A pile of silver coins competed with an equally high jumble of gold ones.

"Welcome to my lair. I'm going to set your jewelry box

here and we'll find a few favorites to fill it. First, I have a tradition. Scoot over there and then come join me."

Baffled and curious, Ciel followed his directions. She turned back around to see the immense silver dragon walk into the middle of the coins and drop to his belly. The floor shook from the impact. Her jaw dropped open as he rolled on the coins, scattering them in a delightful tinkling sound.

*Come, Little Sky. Have fun on your birthday.*

A giggle burst from her lips and Ciel ran forward to climb up to the top of the silver coins. She sat down, feeling like the queen of the hill. Giving into an impulse, she pushed off and slid on her bottom, riding a cascade of money. She couldn't contain her laughter at the crazy way to enjoy his money. Finally at the bottom, she stretched out on her back. Ciel grabbed handfuls of coins next to her and let them cascade to the floor.

Argenis nudged a small pile her way before resting his head on his horde and inhaling deeply as he watched her. His shiny silver scales reflected the glow from the lights. He actually blended in with the treasure in a few places.

Sitting up, Ciel scooted over to sit next to his head. The coins below her were cold for an instant or so and then warmed. Ciel reached out a hand to slide over his scales on his head. His eyes closed partially, and that deep rumble escaped once again. She didn't comment on it. Ciel had already discovered that Argenis only made that sound when he enjoyed life. It made her smile. She loved that he shared this private joy with her.

An image flashed into her brain of Argenis in human form, poised between her thighs with his cock pressed against her needy core. Heat burst inside her at the erotic sight. She squeezed her legs together as she felt her juices drench the purple panties she wore.

His massive head rose slightly. She felt her face flame hot as he inhaled the scent of her desire. A quick snort produced another smoke heart. Pressing her hands against her thudding heart, she blew him a kiss.

In a shimmer, he reverted to his human form. Argenis reached forward and wrapped his arms around her, pulling Ciel onto his lap. He cupped her face and kissed her deeply.

When he lifted his head, Ciel blinked a few times before asking, "Do you want to make love here?" she said, waving a hand over the pile they sat on.

"No way. The coins are fine on dragon scales but tough on the skin. I'll get a blow-up mattress to cushion my old bones."

"Good idea. You are ancient."

"Your bottom is begging for that birthday spanking, isn't it?"

She shook her head rapidly, reassured only by his smile that she hadn't hurt his feelings.

"Come on, birthday girl. Let's go see what you'd like to put in your jewelry chest."

It had to take her an hour to look through the earrings alone. She tried not to take too many, but there were five pairs she couldn't live without. Ciel had to admit that the jewelry box looked happier with some sparkles in it.

"Tiara?" He tempted her with a lovely one set with twinkling diamonds

"Maybe someday? Right now, could you take me on a ride?"

"Dragon flight?" he asked.

"Yes, please. Just up in the clouds." She didn't know why but up in the air all the worries and difficulties disappeared.

"I would enjoy that, too. Let's put this in our room."

He closed the top of her jewelry chest and hoisted it back

118

onto his shoulder. Taking her hand, he led her to the thick door.

"Hmm," he hummed as he looked back at the treasure hoard.

"Something wrong?"

"Just deciding on the size of that air mattress," he said and winked at her as he ushered her through the door.

"You!" she said, laughing.

"You love me," he told her with a fond look as he relocked the door with one hand.

"I do," she answered quietly.

Immediately, he turned to look at her.

"I do love you," she repeated.

Discarding the jewelry case on the floor, he wrapped his arms around Ciel. Argenis lifted her off her feet and whirled Ciel around in a circle before kissing her hard.

"Say it again," he demanded.

"I love you, Daddy."

"I love you, Ciel. Fair warning, you'll have to tell me that at least once a day or I'll get grumpy."

"Heavens forbid. A grumpy dragon? I'll make sure to avoid that. I could make a sign?" she teased.

"Or just tell me frequently," he suggested.

"Yes, Daddy."

"Good girl. Let's go for a flight."

# Chapter 16

After her momentous birthday when Argenis spent the whole day with her, he'd had to return to patrol. She tried not to demand too much of his time, but she wanted all of it. Today, she'd wandered outside, hoping to see the dragons flying overhead.

"I'm bored, Silly," Ciel admitted to her stuffie as she enjoyed the breeze outside. Even though things had been so much easier before, she adored her new life with Argenis. She'd never felt this way about anyone—much less told them.

But her mate had an enormous responsibility now. Protecting everyone inside the ring of mountains took time and vigilance.

Restless, she hopped out of the swing on its next forward arc. Instantly, she heard a knock on the large window on her mate's office. *Sorry!*

"I can't do anything," Ciel muttered aloud. She flounced down to sit on the green grass and gasped. Her mate had spanked her soundly when they returned from the excursion. Not following directions and being bratty had earned her a very different type of spanking from her first. Ciel's bottom was still sore.

"I'm going to be good forever now, Silly. No more rolling my eyes at Daddy or trying to run around him."

Ciel tried to listen to Silly's wise advice to follow her Daddy's directions, but her mind replayed the information Argenis had shared with her at breakfast.

Just yesterday, the man who'd managed the livestock on his land for years had stopped a group of men carrying tools at the base of the mountain. They'd all answered questions correctly, reporting they'd recently been allowed over the mountain passes to work in Wyvern. That week, they'd been assigned to remove the large stones from an unused field to get it ready for planting. The men were camping out near the area. According to Argenis, the sight of shovels and pickaxes had thrilled the supervisor. They'd even had a hoe.

Something in the men's story seemed off. What they said was perfectly logical. But...

Argenis trusted his long-term employee. His father and grandfather still lived and worked on the estate. Argenis shared with Ciel that visiting these men was on his list to do that day.

"Just in case, stay near the house today," the dragon declared.

He would talk to the new men. Dragons could smell lies. He would take care of any problem or clear the haze of wariness away.

Ciel knew from her mate's expression, he was concerned. Something was off about these men.

"I was going to help with the cheese making today, Daddy. I'll stay on the path."

"Not today, Little Sky," he'd declared with a look that told her not to argue.

Thus, her boredom. She'd had her day all planned out. Now she was stuck in the house or just outside. There was nothing fun to do.

After debating for several swings back and forth, Ciel dragged her sandals on the ground to come to a stop. Immediately, she reached down to brush away the dust from her pretty silver sandals. Argenis had loved her wearing his color. She liked pleasing him.

A dragon shout echoed through the green space, and she saw Argenis run toward it. In seconds, the silver dragon soared away. With him out of his office, she decided to dare leaving the play area near the house. Ciel tucked Silly inside the back of her shirt and headed down the hill. She'd need both hands to make cheese. *He'll never know.*

"Hi," Ciel greeted the couple in the barn.

"Hi, Ciel. Did you come to sample some cheese?" the woman asked.

"I'd hoped you'd let me help. Is there anything easy I could do? I'd hate to mess something up."

"Of course. We can always use another pair of hands. Today, we're scooping up the curds into a mold and placing weights on them to press out the moisture. Are you feeling strong?" the man asked.

"Sure. Just show me."

Soon, Ciel wore an apron and gloves. It was easy to get engrossed in the process. She got the knack of how to heap the curds into the mold so that when she set the weight on top, they would be full. It was messy work and she loved it.

"Good job, Ciel! Thank you for your help. We got everything done so fast today, we can get the vat cleaned and set up for another type of cheese tomorrow," the woman praised her.

"I can help with that," Ciel rushed to volunteer.

"Thank you, but that's a two-person job. You're welcome back any other time to help us," the man said with a smile.

"Okay." Taking her apron and gloves off, Ciel laid them neatly on the counter. On her way back to the mansion, she stopped to watch the baby goats. They were so cute bouncing around.

Grinning, she turned to go back up the incline. She was almost there when she ran into a group of men.

"That's her. That's the silver dragon's mate," the rough man announced.

Just the sight of them warned her that they were up to no good. She opened her mouth to scream, but they were on her before she could let out a peep. She concentrated with all her might and screamed one word in her mind as they gagged and tied her up.

*Argenis!*

One man threw her over his shoulder, and they ran toward the rocks. He jerked her off his shoulder and thrust her toward the side of the mountain. Were they going to bash her against the stone? She dug the toes of her shoes into the ground trying to slow herself down and felt one sandal rip off her foot.

*Where are...*

She closed her eyes anticipating pain and felt the bite of rocks scraping the skin of her back and front. Flashing her eyelids open, she discovered she was being pushed inside a very narrow opening. As she emerged on the other side, someone held her roughly. Then the same man grabbed her and threw her back onto his shoulder.

The rest of Argenis's worried response never arrived as they dashed into a tunnel hidden in the craggy rock. The man carried her deeper and deeper into the darkness lit only by flickering torches. The others extinguished the light behind them.

Finally, one spoke. "Surely, he can't hear us here."

"You going to guarantee that?" another asked.

"Put her in the box," the first one directed.

At the sight of what looked like a big footlocker, Ciel fought the rough ropes tied around her wrists and ankles. It did no good. Soon, the top slammed into place and she heard the latches lock into place.

*Argenis!*

There was no response.

*Daddy?*

When that also was met with silence, Ciel panicked and tried to shift over onto her back. Landing on the soft stuffie she'd tucked into her shirt a few hours ago, she froze. Silly was here. Ciel concentrated on getting her breathing under control. She wasn't alone. Argenis was coming. He'd find her if he had to destroy the whole mountain.

"Something's happened. I have to get home." Argenis threw the words over his shoulder as he ran for a clearing.

Shifting into a dragon, he launched himself into the air. A flash of emerald green told him another dragon was coming with him in case he needed backup.

*Someone has taken Ciel,* he mentally sent to Khadar.

A flash of anger that rolled through his mind was the only response Argenis received. He agreed with that completely. Whoever had taken her had just sealed their fate.

The dragons landed behind the house and Argenis raced toward the last place he'd heard her call. They scoured the area along with staff members. Retracing his steps repeatedly, Argenis found nothing.

He stopped and tried to think. Khadar joined him as well as a ring of others. "Her voice stopped mid-thought. She either was gagged or shielded from connecting with me."

"What would interrupt your connection?" Khadar asked. "A thick barrier?"

"It would have to be made of a solid material."

"We build our lairs into the side of the mountain to protect from fire but also so we can not be spied on," Khadar suggested.

"Or even have someone know you existed," one man added. The townspeople were still astonished that they had no idea about the dragons other than the statue in the square.

An image of the used tools flashed into Argenis's mind. "They're inside the mountain."

"There's no way you didn't hear them excavating your mountain," Khadar scoffed.

"Unless they only worked when I was out. Put one man on my staff for a look out and they would know when I appeared and flew out immediately," Argenis said, feeling the anger build inside him.

Khadar's expression hardened. "That would work."

"There are caves in several places but three main entrances. I have barricaded all with boulders," Argenis reported. "Let's check those openings."

He divided the men in two, before waving them in opposite directions. Khadar joined the smallest group to reinforce them. On his own, Argenis headed down the hill. As he passed the cheese makers' new building, a woman called out.

"Thank Ciel for us. She could be a master craftswoman."

"Ciel was here?"

"Yes. She was wonderful."

Argenis immediately ran for the last entrance. The boulders were all still in place. There was no way anyone had moved those massive pieces of rock without having machinery or dragon power. He would have noticed both. He slammed his hand into a large jutting section of stone. She couldn't just disappear. He paced further down the slope. A flash of silver caught his eye. Racing down to investigate, he found Ciel's sandal. He'd noticed it this morning, approving of her choice of colors. She needed to wear more silver.

Scanning the ground, he saw a patch of grass raked and torn. There was nothing else except the craggy rock that formed his mountain. Wait! There! A patch of rock lay scattered by a jagged section.

Argenis rounded the protrusion and found it. He visually traced the jagged crevice running vertically at the back of the jutting section of rock. It had been widened, just wide enough for a person to squeeze in if they went from a certain angle.

*Khadar, I found where they took her.*

*Go! I know where you are.*

*Bring the men here to guard this entrance.*

# Chapter 17

Forcing himself to stop and listen, Argenis detected the sound of one man's breath. He zeroed in on the sound to find his location. He'd apologize to Ciel later.

*Whack!*

The flat sandal smacked the man's torso as planned. When the guard stashed at the entrance swung his shovel downward to bash anyone who tried to follow inside, Argenis dodged the blow easily and ripped the man through the entrance. Luckily for the bad guy, he struck his head on the jutting rock and was knocked out completely before Argenis could dole out any consequences for the villain's involvement.

Argenis tossed him to the side as Khadar and the other men reached the entrance. "Stay out here and deal will the trash I toss out to you. Don't let anyone get away."

"On it, sir. You can count on us," his supervisor promised.

"Thank you, Albert."

Listening again, he heard nothing. This time, he slipped through the opening. His bulk challenged the narrow opening. Argenis tore chunks of rock away to make room.

The entrance was the only source of light. Argenis paused to let his eyes adjust to the darkness. The darkness would be a challenge for his foes as well. With luck, they didn't know the talent of a silver dragon.

When the passageway branched off in two directions, Argenis eliminated one by smell alone. The stench of fear was coming from the right side. He continued that way.

A narrowing made him hesitate. Argenis wrapped his hand around the wall and discovered the bottleneck led into a wider section. It would be the perfect spot to jump someone. If they weren't a dragon...

Using his senses, Argenis pinpointed two people in the room. From the sound of their racing hearts, he knew they were on the edge of panicking. He blew a long stream of warm air into the room, heating it. Now he could smell them sweating. Their hands would be slippery on their weapons now. Laying his hands on the rocks, Argenis pumped heat into the stone.

The men yelped and dashed to the center of the room to get away from the burning rocks. Sliding through the now unguarded opening, Argenis quickly knocked the men out. He took a few seconds to tie them together with their belts before moving on.

A glow of light appeared before him. This must be the final area. He searched for a trace of Ciel and could feel a tendril of fear. They had her enclosed in something. His anger threatened to overrule his strategic plan. Quickly, he controlled his emotions. She was safe.

Once again, he forced himself to stop and listen instead of rush immediately to her side. Five men filled the area before him, scattered throughout the room.

"This doesn't end well," he called. There was no need to try to sneak up on them. They already knew he was there.

"We'll make a trade. A million in silver coins for your mate," one man answered.

"She is definitely worth that and more. Dragons are selfish creatures. They don't part with treasures."

"You will this time."

The incredible bravado of that response almost made him laugh as his plan to deal with these kidnappers took a fatal turn. There was no way these men would survive today. "You are already dead. You just don't realize it yet."

Restless shifts of bodies answered him. Argenis didn't wait long. He didn't want them to regain their confidence. Wedging himself as far back as he could, Argenis shifted. Completely vulnerable in his position squished into the passageway without the ability to turn or avoid an attack, he concentrated. His scales gathered light from the room in front of him and magnified thousands of times over.

As the intensity grew, it filled all the spaces inside. Khadar would realize what was happening and get his men away from the opening, so they weren't affected. Whatever they had restrained Ciel inside would protect her. If it could stop her thoughts from reaching him, it would stop enough of his light.

One by one, Argenis heard their hearts stop beating. When the last one ceased, he forced the glow to recede. Shifting back into his human shape, he raced through the opening and spotted the box where they'd secured Ciel. He dropped to his knees, quickly dealt with the locks, and threw the lid open.

Ciel huddled cramped inside the small space. With her arms stretched over her eyes, she'd obviously realized what was happening and shielded herself. Her heart rate and breathing were very slow. The tight seal of the locker had restricted the airflow as well. Obviously brought in through the tight passages in pieces and assembled there, the locker contained minuscule gaps in its construction that had allowed him to sense Ciel through the reinforced sides, but over time, she'd consumed the oxygen inside. Especially with panicked breathing.

Argenis knew he had barely gotten to her in time. Biting off a curse, he smoothed a hand over her hair. "Breathe, Little Sky. Daddy's here. You're safe now."

She moved slightly, trying to get closer to him.

"That's it, Ciel. You're safe. Take a deep breath."

"Daddy?" she mumbled.

"I am here. You're okay now. Just breathe." He gathered her into his arms, lifting her out of the confining box to hold her close.

When his hands felt the lump under her shirt, he quickly reached a hand into investigate. "What in the..."

"It's Silly. He was going to pop out and hurt them if they did anything to me."

"I'm sure he would have taken on the whole group. Thank you, Silly for having my mate's back." Argenis pressed Silly into her arms before drawing her close once again. He kissed her temple as he rocked her slowly. Celebrating each movement she made, he gave her the time she needed to recover. When her hand clamped onto his shirt as if she'd never let him go, Argenis knew she'd be okay.

"I've got you, Ciel."

"Could we get out of here?" she asked.

"Are you hurt?" He ran his hands over her arms and legs, mentally cursing the invaders at each of her gasps.

"I can walk. They didn't break anything."

Argenis saw red for a flash and forced himself to control his anger as she deliberately didn't answer his question. He vowed that no one would ever endanger her again. When he was back under control, he spoke to her.

"Yes. I want you to follow Daddy's instructions closely. It may be dark in some places," he warned. "Stay close to me and we'll be outside soon."

"Yes, Daddy," she agreed, nodding enthusiastically.

He could tell she just wanted to be out of the tunnel. Drawing her face forward, Argenis kissed her lightly. "I'm very proud of you, Ciel."

"I knew you'd come. Who takes on a dragon?" she said.

Argenis was glad to hear some of the spunk coming back to her normal attitude. "Who indeed? Let's go. Close your eyes."

When she complied, he stood with her in his arms. Carrying her away from the bodies scattered on the hard stones, he reached the doorway. They would have to go through that one by one. In each section, he lit the torches and extinguished them as they left, except for the one area where he'd bound his two attackers together. His light had finished them. Argenis guided her through that murky area without the torches to prevent her from seeing the men.

When they reached the final doorway, Argenis sent a blast to Khadar. *We're coming out.* He could hear the emerald dragon warning the men who guarded the entrance.

A cheer went up as first Argenis and then Ciel emerged. In the sunlight, he checked her over, finding only scrapes and bruises she'd alerted him to, but no severe injuries. When he was sure she wasn't hiding any injuries from him, Argenis turned to the men who'd backed him up.

"My thanks for ensuring my mate is safe. Know that your place here on my land is secure for generations."

He would thank them with security for their loved ones. Just as they had loaned their strength to protect his mate.

Holding Ciel close to his side, Argenis shook hands with each one and learned their names. He would not forget their help that day.

"If you will forgive me, I will tend to my mate."

Everyone nodded and moved to make a path back to the mansion as Argenis swept her up into his arms. He paused to look at Khadar and sent him a message.

*Would you secure that opening after bringing the bodies out?*

Khadar nodded. *What would you like done with the bodies?*

*Burn them. I owe you one, Khadar.*

*I will count on your assistance when my mate is in danger.*

*You will have it.*

Giving that promise, Argenis turned and strode toward the mansion. He pressed a kiss to Ciel's forehead, concerned by her paleness. "You're safe now."

"I knew I was safe when you arrived. I've been trying to keep score. It's like Dragon at four thousand, seven hundred and twelve to bad guys at zero. You'd think they'd learn a lesson," she said in a light tone.

"You would think. Unfortunately, bad guys in critical situations make even worse decisions."

"Is she okay?" the housekeeper asked, opening the door for Argenis to carry her inside.

"I'm fine," Ciel rushed to assure her. "Argenis just likes carrying me around."

"Abby, would you mind making us a tray for dinner? Something light."

"Of course, sir."

"Thank you, Abby," Ciel called over her mate's shoulder as he carried her away.

134

"You're welcome, ma'am."

"I think a warm bath is in order," Argenis suggested, carrying her through their bedroom and into the large, attached bathroom. He set her on the vanity. "Are you okay here for a minute?"

"I'm fine, Argenis. You don't need to fuss over me."

"Get used to it, mate." He hoped his gentle tone completely erased the bluntness of his words. Having her at risk had taken a few hundred years off his life.

"I'm fine, Argenis. Go start the bath for us."

He kissed her lips softly and stepped away to turn on the tap. Thank goodness the old ways of pumping water had not been completely destroyed. He tossed a handful of healing salts into the water, knowing they would sting her wounds at first, but soothe them while she soaked.

As the water rose, he returned to her side. "Silly will need to stay here. We'll give him a bath later."

She nodded and set the stuffie on the vanity.

"Stand up for me, Little Sky. Let's get these dirty clothes off."

"Can we wash my hair, too? I'm sure there were spiders in there."

"Of course."

Argenis tried not to growl at every scrape and scratch on her body. The hint of bruising would blossom into colors tomorrow. There was no doubt that the men had not cared about his precious mate at all. He wished he could slaughter them all again and make it so much more painful.

"Stop it, Daddy. Whatever you're thinking, push it out of your mind," she ordered, smoothing a finger over his wrinkled brow. "We're home together. It's okay."

"I will try, Little Sky. I don't like seeing you hurt."

He knelt in front of Ciel to remove the one sandal still

strapped to her foot and the clothing bunched around her feet. When he had her stripped, Argenis discarded his garments quickly. He enjoyed seeing the spark of interest in her eyes. They had mistreated his mate, but she was strong and already recovering.

Leading her to the bathtub, he held her steady with one hand as he leaned over the water to heat it. Several short breaths of heat made the aroma of the bath salts perfume the air. After testing it with a swipe of his hand, he lifted Ciel and sat her in the water.

"It hurts," she cried and tried to scramble to get out.

"The sting is gone now, Ciel."

She froze as she took stock of her level of pain before sending a pointed look his way. "It is better now. But it hurt. You didn't warn me."

"Would that have made it better?"

"No," she admitted, leaning back against the side of the tub to wave her hands through the fragrant liquid.

"It could use some more water," she pointed out.

"Not once a dragon gets inside."

"You're coming in, too?" she squeaked as he stepped into the tub.

"Make way... Dragon."

He settled behind her and pulled Ciel back to rest against his chest. He felt her soften against him and he pressed a kiss to her head. "Just relax. I've got you."

He slowly smoothed water over her body, washing away the smudges of grime and cleaning the scrapes and scratches. Holding on to his self-control as he discovered sore spots on her skin, Argenis treated her injuries.

A large crashing sound made the surface of the water quiver. Ciel sat straight up. "What's that?"

"Khadar just sealed the entrance for us."

"What did he do? Take down half the mountain?" she asked with awe.

"I have a feeling he just gave the mountain a tap with his tail. That's what I would have done."

"That was a tap?"

He kissed her shoulder and resumed bathing her.

"That feels so good," she whispered.

"I'm glad, Little one. Let's slide you down to dip your head in the water. I didn't know when I met you, I'd become a world famous spider hunter."

"Spiders are awful," she whispered as he helped her wet her hair.

When she sat back in front of him, Argenis poured shampoo on his hands and lathered her long hair. Scratching her scalp lightly, he assured her, "No spiders, Little Sky."

"They all ran away. Because, you know, Dragon," she teased.

"As they should. Dragons are fiercely protective of those they love."

"Thank you for saving me, Daddy."

"Every time, Ciel. If you call, I'm there. Of course, I may never leave your side again," he warned.

"I'll be okay with that for a while."

"Deal."

# Chapter 18

Argenis felt her relax on his back and knew she'd be asleep soon. His mate had become quite the companion on flights. There were times when he couldn't take her with him, but if he could, she didn't hesitate to go with him.

A woman raised on technology as a babysitter, Ciel was struggling to adjust to not picking up her phone and cruising through social media. The last year, she'd spent studying. It would be a very long time before schools reopened. She needed a new interest.

She'd devoured all the romances in his library. Today, on the way home from patrols, he had a surprise for her. He had a feeling she would be very excited.

A couple of hours later, he felt her wake up. The slight change in their mental connection from her mind in slumber to drowsy and then alert always enchanted him. She hugged his neck. Okay, everything about her delighted him.

*I think I fell asleep.*

*You woke up just in time. Look below.*

She followed the direction he pointed with his massive

head and took a quick breath in. *What's going on? Is there trouble in Wyvern?*

*It's a celebration, Little Sky. Today is a special day.*

*Really? What's happening?*

*You'll have to wait to see. I'll land soon.*

True to his word, Argenis dropped to the ground with a gentle thump. Well used to sliding off her mate now, Ciel dismounted gracefully and stepped back in his line of vision so he could know that she was safe. In a flash, he strode forward to claim a kiss.

"Let's go, Daddy. I can't wait to see what's happening."

They threaded their way through the streets of Wyvern. Running into people as they walked, Ciel stuck by his side. She understood why people kept their distance when they met people she'd known for years. Ciel called it the big, scary dragon effect. She and Aurora had become great friends and confidantes. Argenis knew it was comforting to know that Ciel wasn't the only one that people suddenly reacted differently to because of their mates.

He did not mind being on the outskirts of society. Being alone on his mountain was his favorite place to be. Interacting with people was a necessary task. He would do this for her.

"The library?" she asked, almost dancing with excitement.

"Yes, Little Sky. Today is the grand reopening."

He had timed it perfectly. As they walked up to the edge of the crowd, the town leader cut the ribbon, opening the doors once again. A committee had approached the town council to allow residents to establish regular hours for the building to be open. Taking books on an honor system, anyone could check out two books at a time.

"Did you know?" a familiar voice asked behind her.

"Aurora! I didn't!" Ciel darted toward her friend to hug her before waving at Drake. "BSD," she whispered to her friend, and they both giggled.

Drake rolled his eyes at their merriment, obviously in on the code for Big Scary Dragon. "Go get some books, you two. I have something to discuss with Argenis."

Holding hands, the two women joined the crowd. Connected still by a thread of mental communication, the dragons could keep track of their mates.

"What's going on?" Argenis asked in concern as soon as they were out of earshot.

"Nothing. I just didn't want to go in there," Drake confessed.

"Ah. Good idea."

The two dragons moved a slight distance away, so they didn't intimidate anyone. The foot traffic has shifted away from them, creating a snarl that eased as soon as they had cleared the area. With their backs to a nearby building, they could keep an eye on everything.

A child ran over to stand in front of them, staring. Argenis and Drake returned the careful consideration. Finally, the young boy asked, "Can you dragon out?"

"Simon! Do not bother the dragons. They are keeping us safe." The frazzled mother grabbed his hand. "My apologies, gentle... I mean, dragons. Sir Dragons?" She struggled to know how to address them.

"Dragon is fine. An inquisitive mind is admirable. We are not bothered," Argenis told her before fixing a stern look on Simon. "We do not however, perform like trained ponies and dragon out on request."

The little boy gulped audibly and nodded. "Sorry."

"He's fascinated by dragons, of course. His favorite stuffed animal is a dragon."

"Really? What color?" Drake asked casually.

"Silvery gray."

Argenis's mouth went dry, and he tried not to allow the whirl of thoughts in his mind to show on his face. "That is the best color, of course."

"You're a silver dragon?" Simon asked.

"I am."

"Come Simon. Let's not pester the dragons," his mother repeated as she tugged him away with a thankful smile at Argenis and Drake.

"I wish there were phones again. I could have gotten a picture with them." The young man's voice drifted back to them.

"That doesn't mean anything," Drake assured him the moment they were out of earshot, obviously reading the other dragon's thoughts.

"There is only one mate at a time. That young man was six?" Argenis asked. His mind raced. Was Ciel's life in danger? Was she ill? That couldn't happen again, could it?

"Just because he has a dragon means nothing," Drake said quietly.

"A silver dragon."

"The moment we were back in the spotlight, I'm sure every dragon in the toy store was claimed. It probably means nothing," Drake suggested.

"I know. It's just too... Too close. I can't lose another one so quickly."

"As we both know, even we can't battle fate and win. We also can't live expecting the worst. Would you have ever expected Wyvern to need its dragons so urgently again?"

Argenis considered his words. Drake could be completely right. Or he might just have a few years with Ciel.

"Daddy! I was waving. Didn't you see me?" Ciel said, appearing in front of him.

"The sun must have been in my eyes, Little Sky. Did you find a couple of books?" he asked, gesturing to the ones in her hand.

"I did. These look really good."

"I'm glad, Ciel. Are you ready to go home?"

"Wyvern is having a picnic. Can we stay? They're grilling hotdogs. Everyone brought something to share, but they told us the dragons have done so much, they would be honored for us to join them." Ciel almost danced in her excitement.

"I think we could stay here for a while," he allowed, and both women cheered. "Let me hold those for you. Go socialize. Drake and I will strategize."

A hint of awareness made both dragons turn and step in front of their mates before they could depart. Keres approached. The crowd visibly shrank from the threatening vibes that the black dragon emitted.

"Keres," Argenis acknowledged when the other dragon halted a few steps from them.

"Argenis, Drake, mates. Do you want to introduce me to your mate, Argenis?"

"This is Ciel," Argenis said, not moving a muscle to allow the black dragon to see his mate. A jolt to his back made him automatically reach back to support her.

"Hi, Keres!" Ciel looked over her mate's shoulder as she clung to him in piggyback fashion.

A flash of amusement was stamped down by sadness on Keres's face. The dragon nodded and turned to walk away.

"Did I do something wrong?" Ciel asked.

"No, Little one. Keres battles his own demons. He has been too long without a mate," Argenis assured her.

"I hope he finds a mate soon. The picnic is a great place to search for her or him," Ciel suggested.

"I have a feeling that's what everyone thinks," Drake suggested, nodding to Khadar who approached.

Ciel immediately slid down to the ground and darted around Argenis to go talk to the emerald dragon. Knowing she was safe, Argenis followed her at a more sedate pace.

"Khadar! I'm so glad to see you. Did you whomp the mountain with your tail? That's what Daddy said."

"To close the opening? Definitely. No one's getting in there now," Khadar promised. "And good day to you, Lady Ciel."

"Thank you for helping Daddy rescue me," Ciel told him as Argenis reached them.

"I did very little. Your mate was the hero of the day. I was just there to... whomp," he finished, using her description.

"You did good. I went down there to look. Are you here to look for a mate?" Ciel asked, before slapping a hand over her mouth. "Maybe I shouldn't have asked that."

"It's okay to ask anything. Dragons don't answer anything they don't want to," Khadar told her.

Argenis watched the emerald dragon's words compute in Ciel's brain. He had not answered her question about a mate. Wisely, she nodded.

"Have you met my friend Aurora?" Ciel changed the subject as Drake and Aurora joined them.

"I have met the gold dragon's mate. My greetings, Lady Aurora."

"Hi, Khadar. It's good to see you again," Aurora greeted him.

"I see you all have found some spicy reads," Khadar observed.

"Those are ours," Aurora rushed to clarify why the dragons were carrying romance novels.

"A smart dragon always reads what his mate reads. It's usually very enlightening," Khadar suggested. "If you will excuse me, I might need to check out a couple of books."

"They're having a picnic this afternoon. Dragons are invited," Ciel rushed to tell him.

"Thank you, Lady Ciel." With a nod, he walked into the crowd.

"He has such pretty, old-world manners," Aurora commented.

"He is the charmer among us. The other unmated dragons are here as well," Argenis shared.

"How many hotdogs can a dragon eat? Maybe we should get some hotdogs from home," Ciel suggested.

"We will make sure there is enough food, Little Sky," he assured his mate.

Chapter 19

Waking up wrapped in her mate's arms was the best thing, Ciel decided. She pressed a kiss to his broad chest. "Morning!"

"You are waking up in a good mood," he said, squeezing her close and inhaling deeply as if scenting her.

Ignoring that new trend of smelling her, Ciel answered, "Of course. I slept very well." After he exhausted her with orgasms, she'd slept like a log.

"Perfect. My bedtime story worked well."

Ciel felt her face flame with heat. "You are bad."

"I'm referring to the chapter in the book we are reading together. What are you talking about?"

"Daddy!" Now she was even more embarrassed. She'd thought he was talking about making love to her. Ciel tried to keep her thoughts from replaying his masterful skills.

She seized on his reference. They were reading her books together. His deep voice made the words come alive more than ever before—especially when they came to a spicy scene. Ciel was sorry all her age play books had been on her e-reader. They were lost to her. She couldn't imagine hearing him read one of those.

"You're thinking awfully hard," he observed.

"Sorry. I was just sorry I didn't have all my books in paperback form."

"Some books other than those in the library?"

"Yes. My... You know. My Daddy books," she admitted.

"Why don't you write one for us to read?"

"I'm not an author," she protested.

"Why not? What is it that makes an author, an author?"

"They've written a book?"

"So..." His voice trailed off.

"There aren't any computers," she reminded him.

"There might be a dragon in this bed who has a manual typewriter in his lair."

"You really are a hoarder, aren't you?" she teased.

"A collector of all things valuable," he corrected with a smirk.

"It might be fun to try. Not that I could really do it, but I really don't have anything to do."

"You do many things. The cheese crafters brag about your skills. I'm not railroading you in to writing a book. I'm just making that possible if you're interested. Now, I think there might be something I'm interested in."

She watched as Argenis lifted the sheet over them and ducked under the covers. He trailed kisses down her torso, pausing to swirl her nipples in his mouth. Weaving her fingers in his hair, she caressed his scalp as he moved lower. As his mouth closed over her pussy, Ciel felt her eyes roll upward.

*Daddy!*

He nibbled and licked as if he wanted to stay there all morning. The vibrations of his hums of pleasure pushed her pleasure higher and higher. The feel of his mustache and beard added an extra boost to all the sensations he lavished on her. *Damn, he's good at that!*

*Thank you.*

She shook her head at his response. He did not eavesdrop on her thoughts, but Ciel tended to broadcast when aroused. And he was way too good at that. At everything.

All the whirling sensations built until she didn't care what she shared with him. With a cry, she exploded into a massive orgasm. He coaxed every bit of excitement from Ciel before rekindling her arousal. When his mouth lifted from her clit before she could climax again, Ciel blurted, "No!"

"Don't tell Daddy, no," Argenis chided as he emerged from the bedding.

"But I was almost there. Meanie!"

"And calling Daddy names? You are off to a naughty start, Little Sky," Argenis warned.

The stern voice made her rebel. It wasn't her fault. "Don't be a jerk."

"That's it, Little one."

Before she knew what was happening, Argenis flipped her over on to her hands and knees. He wrapped an arm around her waist, holding her in that position when her first move was to flatten herself to the bed.

"I think your attitude needs some adjustments. You tell me when you can talk nicely to your Daddy." His hand landed on her bottom in quick, stinging swats.

Ciel could feel her skin heating. She wiggled, trying to get away, but Argenis held her firmly in place.

"Mates who talk back to their mates earn consequences."

"I don't like this consequence," she yelled at him.

"That means it's working. Spread your legs apart."

Careful to not add more infractions to her punishment,

Ciel followed his instructions and earned a quick tickle that made her gasp and push back against his fingers. When that touch switched from caresses to punishment, the sting developed into a stronger sensation. Ciel closed her eyes as her arousal roared back to life. She didn't understand how spanking made her hot. The dominance of her mate made everything sexy.

"Do you have anything to say to your Daddy?" he asked when she was close to another orgasm.

"What?"

"Did you forget how you earned this spanking?"

Searching her brain, Ciel tried to come up with the right answer as he continued to pepper her bottom with swats. Tears began to drip from her eyes onto the sheet below her. Unable to think, she went with something that could apply to anything.

"I'm sorry, Daddy."

"That's my good girl."

She felt him shift behind her, moving between her thighs. He thrust into her body, filling her so completely, the air in her lungs gushed from her lips. Desperately, she inhaled as she tried to withstand the sensations his thick shaft created. Her control shattered and Ciel screamed her pleasure into the room and fell to her forearms.

Argenis didn't hesitate. He powered into her over and over, pushing her arousal to levels she'd never thought were possible. When she thought she'd never survive another climax, he growled into her ear.

"With me, Little Sky."

Her body launched into one more burst of incredible bliss as he increased his speed. She heard his shout fill the room and then blackness took over. Ciel was vaguely aware of him gathering her back into his arms a brief time later.

The sweet kisses on her temple made her heart ache with love.

"I'm going to apologize more often," she mumbled as she squirmed into a comfortable position against his hard body. His rumbling laughter that jostled her head pillowed on him didn't bother her at all. She was asleep in seconds.

When her eyes blinked open, sunlight filled the room. Ciel stretched, feeling slight aches from his lovemaking last night. She deliberately stayed on her tummy, knowing she'd feel that spanking for the day at least. The evening replayed in her mind, putting a smile on her face.

His idea that she could write stories flashed into her mind. Argenis certainly had figured out her sexual needs. He was unlike any man she'd ever had a relationship with. Not just sexually, but in how he took care of her and made her the center of his world. She could picture Argenis patting himself on the chest and reminding her he was a dragon. It was more than that.

He cared for her more than anyone had. She knew that he loved her with all his heart. Her worries of his previous mates had disappeared. From what she'd observed, dragons had no desire to interact with others—except their mates. Then they never forgot any they loved. Argenis focused completely on the now. On the relationship he had now. On her.

Rolling onto her side, she wrapped her arms around herself. How had she gotten so lucky to be his mate?

"Good morning, Little Sky."

"Daddy," she said, lifting her arms to request a hug.

To her delight, he wrapped his arms around her and took

a seat on the side of the bed, holding her close. He pressed a fiery kiss to her lips. When he lifted his mouth from hers, he gently brushed her tousled hair back from her face. "Now, it will be a good morning."

"Wear some of your new earrings today," he suggested.

"Are we going somewhere special?" she asked eagerly.

"Not today, Ciel. You don't need an excuse to wear something that makes you happy," he pointed out.

"I know." She laid her cheek against his chest, enjoying having him to herself.

When she heard him inhale, she leaned away. "Why do you keep sniffing me? Do I smell?"

"Only of the very best things. Sex and sweetness underneath."

"Is that a dragon thing? To sniff people? I knew dogs sniffed people."

Affront covered his features. "Dragons do not sniff things like simple-minded dogs."

"Dogs are smart. They can track lost people. Can help people with mobility problems... Or the blind. They can even sense when illnesses are coming like a seizure."

Something in his face made her pause. "That's it, isn't it? You're checking to see if I'm sick. Like your previous mate."

"Ciel," he began, but she interrupted.

"Are you smelling something? Am I going to die?"

"No, Little Sky. Your scent is young and healthy. I cannot sense anything wrong with you."

"Then you need to stop. We have however long we have. We need to make the most out of every day. I will kiss you goodbye every time you leave, and I don't allow myself to think about all the things that could happen to you."

He stared at her before nodding. "You are much wiser than I am, Ciel."

"I doubt that seriously. But I love you—whether we have fifty years or fifty days. I'm going to enjoy every one."

"I love you, Little Sky."

"Then give me another of those yummy kisses that make my toes curl and go make sure Wyvern is safe."

That kiss almost made her beg him to stay. She felt her lips curve in satisfaction at the hungry look on his face. He was voracious. *Rwahr!*

"That is not what I sound like when I roar."

"In my mind it is," she answered pertly.

"I drew a bath for you. Let me reheat it so you can soak your tender parts. Then wear a pair of your earrings and visit the library today." He lifted her to stand next to the bed.

"Yes, sir, Daddy, sir!" she saluted and earned a quick swat to her behind that made her gasp and promise, "I'll be good."

"Just be yourself, Ciel. That's all I ask you to be, Little Sky."

"Deal!"

# Chapter 20

After grabbing a piece of hot bread slathered in freshly made butter and a glass of milk for breakfast, Ciel headed for the library. She sat in Argenis's large leather chair and rubbed her hands over the polished desktop, fighting the urge to stretch out on it. Glancing around, she took in the grandeur of the room, with all the gleaming wood panels and bookshelves.

Her eyes widened. There in a patch of sun near a large window, sat a desk that hadn't been there before. She jumped to her feet and hurried over. A smaller version of his desk, the newest addition, held an old-fashioned typewriter. Ciel pressed a key tentatively. The smack of the key against the roller made her jump. Who needed one of those fancy clicky-clack keyboards?

Taking a seat in the smaller leather chair, she opened the drawers and found a supply of pens and pencils in the middle drawer and paper in one on the side. There was a leather-wrapped journal that was so soft to her touch. It would be a perfect diary.

Why hadn't she thought of logging all the events when

the change had occurred? Probably because she was too occupied with getting home and then adjusting to being a dragon's mate. She opened it and hesitated.

She could use it to gather her thoughts for the book Argenis had suggested she write. She knew Aurora loved the same books she did. If it didn't suck too bad, she bet her friend would enjoy reading a spicy age play story. If Ciel was brave enough to share it.

Grabbing a pen from the drawer, she pressed the notebook flat and started brainstorming. She didn't want to write about dragon Daddies. That was too close. Aurora would suspect that every sex scene she wrote was about her and Argenis's activities.

Could she write a sex scene? Of course she could. She had the best inspiration.

Maybe she'd just start with regular people with normal qualities. Well, larger than normal measurements for some things. Giggling, she decided to set the story back in the time that technology worked. At the beginning, everyone expected the breakdown to be short-lived. Now weeks later, if the lights suddenly went on, it would spark a big celebration because it was so unexpected. Everyone seemed to have accepted that this was their new reality.

Pushing the negative thoughts from her mind, she sketched out a rough plot idea. Her pen flew over the paper as she tried to capture all the tidbits that jumped into her mind. When she sat back in her chair, she looked at all the notes she'd taken. It sounded great. She wanted to read that story.

Ciel glanced at the typewriter next to her. That would be the next challenge. How did she even put the paper in that thing? Paper did fit somewhere inside, right?

"Want me to show you?" Her mate's deep voice made her look over at his desk.

How long had he been there?

"Argenis?" she asked, looking at him in confusion.

He stood and walked toward her. "You've been at it for a few hours. I was just about to stop you for a lunch break."

Her stomach growled at the thought of food. Ciel slapped a hand over her stomach to muffle the sound.

"Second thought. Lunch first. Typewriter conquest later." He held a hand out for hers and pulled her from the chair. "Did you enjoy your morning?"

"It was so much fun. I had no idea so much time had flown past. How was your morning?"

"Very good. I made a quick stop." He set a small bottle of correction fluid next to the typewriter.

"What's that?"

"It's like fingernail polish but for whiting out mistakes on paper."

"Oh, crap. There's no autocorrect either, is there?"

"There's a dictionary in the bottom drawer," Argenis said with laughter in his beautiful eyes.

"I don't suppose you're a spelling champion, are you?"

"Dragon."

As he ushered her to the door, she peeked up at him. "Does that mean yes?"

"It means superior species."

"How do you spell supercalifragilisticexpialidocious?"

"Dragons don't bother with made-up words."

"You don't know, do you?"

"Not a clue," he admitted easily, making her laugh.

When they sat in the dining room munching on sandwiches and drinking tart lemonade, she invited, "So, tell me what's going on in the world of dragons."

"The town's people have announced a cotillion will be held every year to help the dragons find their mates. They are mandating all single people over the age of eighteen to attend."

"How about a ninety-year-old widow? Does she have to go?"

"She is invited. Everyone in Wyvern is."

"A cotillion? Isn't that a fancy dress dance?"

"I know what you are thinking. Shopping is very limited now. No one will be turned away. In addition, several women's groups have offered to make dresses for anyone who needs something to wear."

"That's nice of them." Her mind immediately went to her wardrobe. She had a couple of nice dresses. She even had a bridesmaid dress that could stand in for a long, fancy party dress. Maybe. It was pretty ugly.

"Abby is already working on something for you. Feel free to talk to her."

"That's so sweet of her. Thanks."

"No gloves," he mandated.

"No gloves?" she repeated in confusion.

His hand reached for hers. Sweeping his fingers over the dragon figure on her skin, he sent a cascade of sensations through her.

"Oh."

"Everyone needs to know that you belong to me."

"I won't look at anyone else."

"You will not," he admitted. "The mate bond is only breakable by death. You are mine."

She couldn't help the corners of her mouth twitching upward. His prehistorical cave dragon claiming was so cute. "You'll have to dance with me then. I love to dance."

"Definitely, you will only dance with me. We will practice after lunch before you dive back into your sexy story."

"What will we do for music?"

"I've got that covered, too."

"Your valuable collector's items?" she teased.

"Exactly. Drink your lemonade. You'll need the sugar boost."

# Epilogue

Ciel stood with Aurora and their dragons on the edge of the dance floor as they waited for the last guests to arrive. Some young people had chosen to view the requirement to attend as a request and not a mandate. Crews of Wyvern citizens were rounding up those who hadn't chosen to attend.

The atmosphere was electric. Not with anger at being delayed or required to come. Those transported to the party quickly helped themselves to a drink and some of the bountiful appetizers. It wasn't often that anyone had time to indulge.

The music coming from the group of talented Wyvern citizen grew louder signaling that the last guest had arrived. Ciel nudged Aurora when an exotic-looking woman in her mid-twenties was escorted into the gathering in her nightshirt. Fuzzy animal slippers on her feet completed the outfit. She looked adorable. As she turned around, Ciel could see the rampant fear on her face.

Instantly, Ciel started forward, followed by Aurora, who must also have seen the same expression on the woman's face. When Argenis tried to stop her, she shook her head and dodged around him, knowing that she would be in big trouble later. The crowd swelled onto the dance floor.

Ciel rose onto her tiptoes to keep the woman in sight. Finally, she reached her side, with Aurora right after her. "Hey. It's okay. I'm Ciel."

"I didn't want to come. They made me." The new arrival's voice shook with emotion and her green eyes welled with tears.

"Everyone is required to be here. It's okay. You can stay with us," Ciel said, waving a hand at Aurora. "You've got two new friends. This is Aurora."

"Lady Ciel. I have this," Abby, their housekeeper, who had made Ciel's dress and many others, said from behind her. She held out a garment. "I brought this just in case. It will fit over her shirt."

"You are a lifesaver, Abby. Here. Let me help you." Ciel and Aurora guided the newcomer's arms into the dress and pulled it around her to belt in the front. It covered her perfectly.

"Thank you," the woman whispered.

"We're glad to help. What's your name?" Aurora asked.

"Lalani."

"What a pretty name."

"Who are those guys?" Lalani asked.

Ciel glanced over her shoulder to see Argenis and Drake positioned behind them. "Those are our dragon mates. They're good guys."

A voice shouted over the hubbub of chatter, announcing that the main buffet was open. The crowd around them surged toward the side of the room, where a delicious aroma emanated. Jostled by the hungry town people, Ciel wrapped her arms around Lalani to keep her with them and felt Aurora hug them both.

The small cluster was drawn away from the dragons, who tried to move through the crowd. A man smelling like he had bathed in whisky bulldozed his way past them to get to the food.

"Oh!" Off-balance, Ciel teetered and fell to her knees. Aurora and Lalani tumbled as well. They clung to each other, trying to get to their feet.

A roar stopped the crowd in their tracks. It was Argenis. A second joined in—Drake. Ciel took advantage of the break from the crush of the group to haul herself and the others to their feet. When a third roar joined the two familiar ones, a shiver of awareness zinged down her spine.

"Who's that?" Aurora asked as Drake and Argenis reached them.

"Me," a deep voice sounded behind them.

Everyone turned to see Khadar take his place around the group. Ciel looked at Aurora, trying to figure out what was going on. An audible inhale of surprise drew her attention back to the young woman they'd just met. She looked at Lalani and up at Khadar. *Could she be...*

"Back to our original protected spot," Argenis ordered. "Khadar, you guard from the rear."

The crowd split to form a space before the two glowering dragons led the way back to the raised dais. Cocooned in the middle, Ciel, Aurora, and Lalani walked easily to the secluded spot. Ciel spotted Abby along the route and snaked a hand out to pull their housekeeper into the protected group.

Once they were past, the crowd resumed their movement to the buffet tables. From her position on the dais, Ciel could see that most weren't out of control or bullying. The sheer number was simply overwhelming.

Argenis wrapped his arms around Ciel and lifted her

from her feet. He pressed his mouth against her ear to growl, "You, Little Sky, will not sit easily for several days."

"I had to help," Ciel tried to excuse herself. She turned to check on Lalani when he set her back on the ground.

Khadar stood in front of the once frightened woman directly in Ciel's view. Even viewing her from the back, Ciel could tell that Kalani stood straighter now as she stared at the massive dragon shifter. A green light flashed from Khadar's eyes and he dropped to one knee in front of Lalani.

"His mate," Ciel whispered.

"So it appears," Argenis confirmed.

# Argenis

Thank you for reading Argenis: Fated Dragon Daddies 2!

Don't miss future sweet and steamy Daddy stories by Pepper North? Subscribe to my newsletter!

Coming soon in the Fated Dragon Daddies series is Khadar: Fated Dragon Daddies 3!

Lalani had just found her birth mother in the secluded town of Wyvern when the change hit. Her joy quickly turned to tears when Lalani lost her to an accident before they could really get to know each other. A clash with a neighboring family makes her withdraw into the big, lonely house. She's not coming out for anything.

Known for his ties with nature, Khadar has taken on the additional role of assisting the townspeople with growing food to sustain them. When he appears at the first gathering featuring some of the crops grown in the community garden, he discovers the most desirable treat of all—his mate.

Change has come to Wyvern. A centuries-old pact between the founders and their powerful allies could save the inhabitants of the city once again, but only a dragon Daddy can truly guard his mate from harm.

## Read more from Pepper North

## Fated Dragon Daddies

Change is coming to Wyvern.
A centuries-old pact between the founders and their powerful allies could save the inhabitants of the city once again, but only a dragon Daddy can truly guard his mate from harm.

## Shadowridge Guardians

Combining the sizzling talents of bestselling authors Pepper North, Kate Oliver, and Becca Jameson, the Shadowridge Guardians are guaranteed to give you a thrill and leave you dreaming of your own throbbing motorcycle joyride.

Are you daring enough to ride with a club of rough, growly, commanding men? The protective Daddies of the Shadowridge Guardians Motorcycle Club will stop at nothing to ensure the safety and protection of everything that belongs to them: their Littles, their club, and their town. Throw in some sassy, naughty, mischievous women who won't hesitate to serve their fair share of attitude even in the face of looming danger, and this brand new MC Romance series is ready to ignite!

## Danger Bluff

Welcome to Danger Bluff where a mysterious billionaire brings together a hand-selected team of men at an abandoned resort in New Zealand. They each owe him a marker. And they all have something in common—a dominant shared code to nurture and protect. They will repay their debts one by one, finding love along the way.

## A Second Chance For Mr. Right

For some, there is a second chance at having Mr. Right. Coulda, Shoulda, Woulda explores a world of connections that can't exist... until they do. Forbidden love abounds when these Daddy Doms refuse to live with regret and claim the women who own their hearts.

## Little Cakes

Welcome to Little Cakes, the bakery that plays Daddy matchmaker! Little Cakes is a sweet and satisfying series, but dare to taste only if you like delicious Daddies, luscious Littles, and guaranteed happily-ever-afters.

## Dr. Richards' Littles®

A beloved age play series that features Littles who find their forever Daddies and Mommies. Dr. Richards guides and supports their efforts to keep their Littles happy and healthy.

Note: Zoey; Dr. Richards' Littles® 1 is available FREE on Pepper's website:
4PepperNorth.club

Dr. Richards' Littles®
is a registered trademark of
With A Wink Publishing, LLC.
All rights reserved.

## SANCTUM

Pepper North introduces you to an age play community that is isolated from the surrounding world. Here Littles can be Little, and Daddies can care for their Littles and keep them protected from the outside world.

## Soldier Daddies

What private mission are these elite soldiers undertaking?
They're all searching for their perfect Little girl.

## The Keepers

This series from Pepper North is a twist on contemporary age play romances. Here are the stories of humans cared for by specially selected Keepers of an alien race. These are science fiction novels that age play readers will love!

## The Magic of Twelve

The Magic of Twelve features the stories of twelve women transported on their 22nd birthday to a new life as the droblin (cherished Little one) of a Sorcerer of Bairn. These magic wielders have waited a long time to take complete care of their droblin's needs. They will protect their precious one to their last drop of magic from a growing menace. Each novel is a complete story.

Pepper North

Ever just gone for it? That's what *USA Today* Bestselling Author Pepper North did in 2017 when she posted a book for sale on Amazon without telling anyone. Thanks to her amazing fans, the support of the writing community, Mr. North, and a killer schedule, she has now written more than 80 books!

Enjoy contemporary, paranormal, dark, and erotic romances that are both sweet and steamy? Pepper will convert you into one of her loyal readers. What's coming in the future? A Daddypalooza!

Sign up for Pepper North's newsletter

Like Pepper North on Facebook

*Argenis*

Join Pepper's Readers' Group for insider information and giveaways!

Follow Pepper everywhere!
Amazon Author Page
BookBub
FaceBook
GoodReads
Instagram
TikToc
Twitter
YouTube
Visit Pepper's website for a current checklist of books!

Made in the USA
Middletown, DE
12 August 2024